DEADLY SEEDS
A WITCH IN THE WOODS

JENNA ST. JAMES

Deadly Seeds

Jenna St. James

❀ Created with Vellum

❧ I ❧

"What are you doing in town?" my cousin, Serena, asked when my porcupine partner, Needles, and I strolled through the front door of her bakery. "I thought you were cataloging on the north side of the island all this week?"

As the game warden for Enchanted Island, it was my job to keep track of all flora and fauna, monitor all water sources, and perform countless other duties. A sharp contrast to the job I used to have as a detective with the Paranormal Apprehension and Detention Agency. But when you retire and move back to your hometown island, and your dad is Black Forest King, you're pretty much guaranteed the job of Game Warden.

"I *am* supposed to be on the north side of the island," I said as I waved to Gertrude Anise sitting by the windows. "But about forty minutes ago, I got a text from Tommy saying he needed to speak to me. It sounded urgent."

My childhood friend, Tommy Trollman, owned a lively bar on the island called Boos & Brews. Tommy was a hulking troll with a wide barrel chest, broad shoulders, beefy hands…and a charming personality.

"Did you want to take him something?" Serena mused as she slid a coffee across the counter to me.

That was the great thing about Serena…she always knew what I wanted. I took a tentative sip of the coffee and smiled. "Yum. What is it?"

"Cherry Blossom Latte. Goes with the cherry scones Tamara and I made this morning for the celebration of the spring equinox. Want some scones?"

"Sounds delicious."

It was just after ten o'clock, and Enchanted Bakery & Brew was still busy. There were seven other customers sitting at tables, talking and eating.

"Are you bringing the cherry scones to the party tomorrow night?" I asked.

"Sure am."

Tomorrow was the first day of spring—the spring equinox—and Dad had invited everyone out to Black Forest for a celebration. There would be about a dozen of us. The only ones in our circle not attending were Tamara Gardener and her fiancée, Zac Sparks, and his little girl, Jayden. They were celebrating with Tamara's large family.

"I got hot cinnamon buns," Tamara called out as three trays hovered over her head. Using her magic, she lowered the trays and slid them inside the display case. "Come and get them while they're hot!"

Chairs scraped across the floor of the bakery as eager customers hurried over.

Serena handed me a large white bag. "Here you go. On the house. Not sure what Tommy will be in the mood for, so I put in two cherry scones, a cinnamon bun, a chocolate-chip cookie, and a caramel-dipped pretzel rod for Needles."

"You're my favorite witch today," Needles said as he leaped off my shoulder and flipped a somersault in the air, his wings glowing purple and green.

Serena and I laughed at his antics.

"You say that every time," I said.

"Because it's true every time," Needles said as he landed on my shoulder.

Needles could only be heard by me and my immediate family and friends…and that was just a recent change of events thanks to two different incidents—one event being wayward magic that happened during an explosion, and the other event happened because of my dad, Black Forest King. With Needles about to go on assignments for PADA with my stepdaughter, Zoie, her boyfriend, Brick, and a Goth forensic scientist named Harlow, Dad felt it imperative for their safety that everyone on the team hear Needles.

So he used his magic and made it happen.

"Tell Tommy I said hello," Serena said.

"Will do." I held up the coffee and bag of goodies. "And thanks, again."

I exited the bakery and climbed into my beat-up Bronco. It was almost as old as I was, had been rolled more times than I could count, and yet it never let me down.

Boos & Brews was just a couple streets over from the bakery, so in no time at all, I pulled into the still-empty parking lot, left my coffee behind but grabbed the bag of goodies, and Needles and I hurried to the front door.

"Tommy didn't say what he wanted?" Needles asked as he landed on my shoulder, his wing brushing my neck.

"Nope. Just that it was urgent he speak with me."

I opened the front door of the establishment and stepped inside. Once my eyes became accustomed, I quickly scanned the room. On any given night, this place was hopping with supernaturals drinking, playing pool, and dancing to the music on the jukebox. But today, in the early mid-morning hours, only staff was inside.

"Tommy's in his office," the bartender called out, tossing Needles a couple pretzels from the bowl on the counter. "He said for you to go on in."

Needles caught the pretzels midair, did two flips, then shoved the pretzels in his mouth, his wings glowing purple and green. *"Now if only I had some rum to wash them down."*

Suppressing the urge to roll my eyes, I nodded to the vampire bartender, then turned and headed for Tommy's office. I'd been in his bar enough to know Tommy was never surprised. The hidden cameras up around the bar made that impossible. Tommy would know I was here before I even knocked on his door.

I knocked anyway.

When he called out for me to enter, I pushed open the door and stepped inside. Grinning, Tommy moved out from behind his desk and engulfed me in a hug. "You look marvelous. Married life is agreeing with you, I see."

"It is. You should try it."

Tommy laughed and patted my back with one of his beefy hands. "I'll pass, my friend." He waved to Needles. "Hello, Needles."

Needles leaped from my shoulder, twirled, bowed, and settled back down on my shoulder...causing Tommy to laugh.

Tommy wasn't just an established entrepreneur. He was also a conscientious money loaner. Or as my sheriff husband, Alex Stone, liked to say—a loan shark with a heart. Basically, Tommy wanted the best for Enchanted Island. So if you came to him with a solid business proposal and the bank wouldn't lend you money...Tommy would. Of course, it would cost a little higher interest than a typical bank loan, but that was the price of doing business, as Tommy was prone to say.

He motioned for me to take a seat across from his desk.

"So what's up?" I asked, handing him the white bag of goodies. "From Serena."

Still grinning, Tommy opened the bag, sniffed, and then groaned. "Is Serena *trying* to fatten me up?"

I laughed. "She said she wasn't sure what you'd like, so she was sending you an assortment."

He closed the bag and set it on his desk. "I'll save them for when I need a sugar boost." He steepled his hands together and leaned back in his chair. "Ella Greenleaf was in last night. She was drinking pretty heavily and unloading her burdens on anyone who would listen. One of the bartenders thought I needed to know, so I went out and had a little chat with her. Seems she's one angry young woman."

I frowned. "Who's Ella Greenleaf? The name sounds familiar."

"She recently opened Teas, Tinctures, & Tonics. I take it you haven't been in?"

I arched an eyebrow. "Seriously? If I can't whip up what we need, then Mom or GiGi can. So, no, I haven't been in."

Tommy grinned. "Let's just say she hasn't had a smooth go of the new business."

"What do you mean?"

"Did she kill someone with a potion?"

I rolled my eyes. "I doubt she killed someone with a potion, Needles."

Tommy laughed. "Not quite that bad. Her first week in business, though, she made a tonic for werewolf shifter, April Howler, to get rid of unwanted hair. Not unusual for female werewolves to want. Unfortunately, there was a mixup in the elixir she was given, and April ended up losing *all* her body hair. From her head, down to her toes."

I gasped. "No! I hadn't heard that."

"Oh, yeah. And that's not the only incident Ella had. Word is she's good at making her own teas and tinctures, but she's had to hire a more experienced witch for the tonics, which is cutting into her costs. You know how new start-ups can be."

I nodded. "I do."

"Anyway, Ella came in last night pretty upset. All but cursing her grandma up one side and down the other."

"Why?"

Tommy leaned in across his desk. "Ella claims Selma Greenleaf, her grandma, has possession of one of the rarest plants in the world—the Lunar Blossom."

Needles shot off my shoulder, his wings turning red and black. *"Selma Greenleaf stole from the north side of the island?"*

My mouth went dry.

There was only one place on the island that the elusive Lunar Blossom grew, and it was on the north side of the island—a place Enchanted Island citizens were not allowed to travel via my dad's order over four hundred years ago.

Most of Enchanted Island was covered in plants, trees, shrubs, and vegetation of some kind. Trees and plants you wouldn't expect to find growing together were commonplace here on our magical island. However, as more and more supernaturals settled on the island, more construction and building had become a necessity—except for the north side. My father refused to let anyone but me and my immediate family and friends roam that area of the island. Every citizen, old and new to the island, knew this rule.

Tommy nodded. "I can see from not only your reaction, but Needles' as well, that there's no way Selma should have ever gotten her hands on the plant."

Needles stopped zipping back and forth across the room and settled back down on my shoulder. Out of habit, I reached over and stroked the tiny porcupine, hoping the connection would keep us both calm.

"Did Ella say how her grandmother got her hands on the Lunar Blossom?"

Tommy shook his head. "No. Ella couldn't get past the fact her grandmother was making her bid on the supply Selma had access to. According to Ella, the plant should be given to her freely. Everyone else could pay, but not her."

"So let me get this straight," I said as calmly as I could. "Selma went onto the north side of the island, stole the Lunar Blossom, and is having supernaturals submit bids to get their hands on it?"

Tommy nodded. "That's how it sounded to me. Ella specifically said everyone else could bid on it, but she should get at least one of the flowers from the plant for free."

"And who is everyone?" I demanded.

"I'm sorry, Shayla. I have no idea." He softened the blow by winking at me. "That's your department, Game Warden."

"Oh, ha-ha."

Tommy grinned and leaned back in his chair. "As the game warden for the island *and* having a father who is a Genius Loci, I'm sure you know the ramifications of some novice getting their hands on the powerful plant."

I nodded. "Yes. The plant has myriad uses, and every aspect of it can be used from its leaves to stem to flower."

Tommy shrugged and lifted his hands. "I don't know about specifics, but I *can* tell you this…if the rumors I've heard over the years are true, what it can do for alcohol alone is worth a pretty penny."

I frowned. "For alcohol? Okay, I know what the plant can do medicinally, but I've not heard about it working with alcohol. What will it do?"

"One drop of the flower's extract can make a drink three times as potent as it should be. A bar owner could put just a couple drops in a bottle and then water the drinks down and still make one bottle last triple the amount of time." Tommy spread his arms wide. "I don't have it, Shayla. And I wouldn't want it, either. Something that powerful, I get the feeling there might be health ramifications later on down the line for the person ingesting. No way something that powerful doesn't have a warning label on it." Tommy leaned forward again, the upper half of his hulking body looming over me. "But a bar owner in trouble might go to great lengths to get his hands on this."

I knew immediately what Tommy was saying to me… without saying it aloud.

"Who? I know you're trying to beat around the bush, Tommy. Who don't you want to say?"

Tommy sighed and leaned back in his chair. For a few seconds, he said nothing. "I know for a fact Donald Frasier is having financial troubles. He has a bar that caters mostly to werewolves on the east side of the island. Of all the bar owners I know, he'd be the one eager to get his hands on the Lunar Blossom."

"What time was Ella in here last night?" I asked.

"I'm way ahead of you. I dug out her receipt for you." He picked up a small slip of paper off his desk and handed it to me. "Looks like she left around 11:00."

"Thanks, Tommy. I appreciate this information."

Tommy winked and stood. "Gotta watch out for one of my oldest friends, don't I? Give my best to your husband."

"Do we have to?" Needles asked, giving me a cheeky grin.

2

I looked up where Teas, Tinctures, & Tonics was located on my interactive map of the island. Luckily, Jordan Owlman kept it updated regularly, and the new store was on there. Parking in front of the shop, I hopped out and waited for Needles to land on my shoulder before striding to the wooden door.

The sound of witches' bells rang out, announcing our arrival.

"Welcome to Teas, Tinctures, & Tonics," a young, dark hair girl called out in a bored voice. Her long locks cascaded over her round shoulders, framing her face and her black glasses. Her curvy body was wrapped in an apron adorned with dancing mushrooms—cute and fresh. I guessed her to be in her early twenties. "Have a look around. Let me know if you need any help." She turned and went back to shoving glass jars on the shelves.

"There's a lot going on in here," Needles said. *"My eyes are starting to hurt."*

I suppressed a smile as I strode deeper into the store. It wasn't large by any stretch of the imagination, but every space was filled and utilized. The walls were lined with wooden shelves that reached the ceiling and were packed with glass jars and bottles of various shapes and sizes. As I stopped to read a jar, I noticed each container was labeled with a handwritten tag describing the contents inside.

"I like the personal touch," I said to Needles.

Soft, warm light from hanging lanterns and floating candles illuminated the space, providing a cozy and homey feel. Even the floor was charming, with its wooden planks and homemade rugs. The air smelled like the herbs, flowers, and spices laid out in the store, and I found I enjoyed the combination.

In a corner dedicated to teas, a large, antique wooden table invited customers to sample different brews. Above it, a chalkboard listed the teas of the day, along with their magical properties and benefits.

Turning to the other side of the store, I smiled when I saw an older witch sitting behind a short counter. She looked to be half asleep. Above her, the sign read "Tonics & Elixirs" in bright red. I immediately remembered Tommy's story of Ella's earlier troubles with a werewolf shifter.

Bypassing the counter, I strode over to where the young girl who'd greeted us stood, straightening the jars she'd just added.

"Excuse me," I said. "Are you Ella Greenleaf?"

She turned and ran her eyes up and down my body, somehow managing to look down her nose at me, even though I was taller. "Yes, I'm Ella. What do you need help with?" She sighed exasperatingly. "Let me guess? You want to cover the gray that's showing? Or maybe those wrinkles around your eyes are finally starting to bothering you? Not to worry. I have something you can drink for your dry, wrinkled skin, and then you can make a paste with the loose tea leaves and apply it to your hair as well. The gray is just a temporary fix, mind you. You may need to glamour that yourself." She reached over and gave me a small, placating smile as she patted my arm. "Or just do yourself a favor, ma'am, and splurge on a trip to the salon. I'm sure you deserve it, no matter what anyone else says."

I was momentarily stunned silent. Of all the things I thought she'd say...never did I think she'd outright insult a potential customer. And as far as she knew, that's exactly what I was.

"How dare you!" Needles zipped off my shoulder, his wings glowing crimson red as he whipped out two quills from his back and waved them back and forth, slicing the air in his anger. *"No one speaks to the princess like that."*

"Yo, chill!" Ella raised both hands in the air and stepped backward. "Get your animal under control, lady, before I ask you to leave."

"Okay," I said, "I think we got off on the wrong foot. How about we try this again? Needles, put your sharp, deadly weapons down before you accidentally cut out her offensive tongue."

At this, Ella's eyes went wide...and Needles chuckled.

With one last warning *swoosh!* of his quills, Needles flew back to my shoulder, his wings still glowing red.

"I think I'll keep ahold of them, Princess. Just in case."

"My name is Agent Loci-Stone. I used to be a detective with PADA." I paused to let that bit of information sink in before pointing to my uniform. "Now I'm the game warden for Enchanted Island. Maybe you know my husband? Sheriff Alex Stone?"

The young woman swallowed, and I could see the apprehension in her eyes even as she shook her head and tried to look unaffected by my announcement. "No. I don't believe I've met either one of you personally."

I smiled tightly. "Well, now you have. This is my partner, Needles. He doesn't take kindly to threats or disrespect...to him or me." I left my smile fall. "Now, let's talk about the Lunar Blossom. Word on the street is your grandmother has gotten her hands on it."

"Them," Ella said. "Granny told me she has a bunch of them."

"That can't be," I said. "There's only one plant on the entire island."

The girl smirked. "Maybe you don't know the island as well as you think, because Granny told me last night she had a cluster of the plants ready to go."

Needles stiffed, his sharp claws digging into my shoulder.

I rushed on before Needles could go all...well, Needles on her. "And she's going to sell these plants to the highest bidder?"

Ella narrowed her eyes and crossed her arms over her chest. "Maybe."

I needed to rethink my line of questioning. Or rather, *how* I was questioning. Ella's ego needed stroking. And while I may hate to do it, it was worth it to get the answers I needed. "I'm just surprised, is all. I can't believe she'd make her own flesh and blood bid for something right along with virtual strangers. I mean, even if she gave you just one measly flower, right? Why make you jump through the hoops like the others?"

Ella threw up her hands. "I know! Can you believe Granny told me I had to bid on the plants like everyone else?" She stamped her foot on the ground. "I'm her granddaughter!"

"Exactly," I said. "Do you know who you are bidding against?"

Ella shrugged. "I don't know. I didn't ask. I just know she harvested the plants last night under the full moon, and she's selling them off today."

"You haven't spoken to or seen your grandmother today?"

Ella shook her head, her long dark locks falling around her

shoulders. "Nope. She didn't come to the table for breakfast this morning. I figured she was out late last night and needed to sleep in."

"So you can't even guess who you'll be bidding against today?" I pushed a little harder.

"I saw Granny fighting with Regina Hawthorn last night in our front yard, so maybe her?"

I knew Regina Hawthorn. I'd given her a citation a year ago for unauthorized harvesting of a protected magical herb. She was not a scrupulous witch by any stretch of the imagination.

"What time was this?"

Ella shrugged. "I don't know. We'd just finished eating, so I'd say around 7:00 or 7:30. I asked Granny what Regina wanted when she came back inside. She just cackled and said she wanted the Lunar Blossom, but she had to be like everyone else, including me, and bid for that privilege. Pissed me off, so I left and came into town to hang out at a couple bars because why the hell not? It beat staying at the house and listening to Granny go on and on about how rich she was going to be when the highest bids came in."

"Did your grandmother tell you where she'd found the Lunar Blossom?"

"Where the moon kisses the water," Ella said.

"Luna Lagoon?" Needles mused.

I nodded. "Sounds like it."

"What's that?" Ella asked.

"Nothing. She said she had plants, as in more than one?"

"Yeah. What good would one plant do her?"

I did my best to ignore her snark…but a part of me wanted to give Ella a good zap for being so lippy and disrespectful. "When was the last time you saw or spoke to your grandmother?"

"Last night. I just told you I left when she started getting all giddy about how rich she was going to get."

"I don't like this one at all," Needles said. *"Can I run her through with one of my quills? Please, Princess? Just one?"*

"There's only one place on the island to get Lunar Blossom, and that's the north side of the island." I leaned in close and looked Ella in the eyes. "And I'm sure I don't need to remind you that no one is to venture onto the north side."

Ella crossed her arms over her chest and shrugged. "You're wrong. Granny said she found it where the moon kisses the water, and I believe her. Why would she lie about that?"

"I'm about to go question her to find out," I said. "Would she still be home this morning?"

"I guess so. It's not like she has a job or anything. Last thing she said to me last night when I was leaving was she'd call me today when she was ready for me to come out to the house and bid on the plants." She scowled and dropped her arms. "I'll never be able to pay the price she'll get from the others. It's *so* not fair!" She stamped her foot again on the ground like a petulant child. "I'm her granddaughter, not some stranger!"

I handed Ella a business card. "When Selma calls, make sure you call me."

Ella reached out and snatched the card from my hand. "Yeah, whatever."

3

When we reached the Bronco, I brought Selma Greenleaf's address up on my app.

"She's on the north side of town," I said, pulling onto the street. "I think I'd like to drive out to Luna Lagoon first and see if I can't find this supposed cluster of Lunar Blossoms for myself. Then we can go question Selma."

"Throw me a pretzel, would ya, Princess? I need to keep up my strength. I'm about to die of starvation back here."

I rolled my eyes but reached into my backpack and tossed him back two pretzels.

Luna Lagoon was a twenty-acre body of water near the center of the island just south of the magical river that cut through Enchanted Island, separating most of the north from the rest of the island. At just the right angle, the moon actually looked like it was reaching down and kissing the water. When that happened, the aurora fish would float to the surface and come out to play—their iridescent bodies being instantly charged with a bioluminescence that caused the fish to look like the aurora borealis. Luna Lagoon was the only place on Enchanted Island that housed that particular school of fish.

"It's beautiful out here." I waited until Needles flew out of the Bronco before grabbing my backpack and shutting the driver's side door. "I love the sound and the smell."

I'd driven us as close as I could to the lagoon, and even though it was still another one-hundred-yard hike, I could already hear the lagoon birds and waterfall calling to me.

It didn't take long for Needles and me to push aside the last of the lush foliage and step into the tranquil oasis that made up Luna Lagoon. The humidity had spiked the moment I'd stepped foot inside the secluded area. Sunlight danced on the surface of the water, causing it to reflect back like a mirror. I walked to the edge, bending down to touch the reeds and water lilies lining the outer border of water.

"It's beautiful, isn't it?" I mused.

"It's what the island used to look like before all the supernaturals came and the houses and building went up."

I knew the history of Enchanted Island, of course. A little over four hundred years ago, a handful of witches had cried out for help and sanctuary from the humans persecuting not only witches, but other supernaturals as well. A real-life witch hunt was taking place, and many were dying. My father, Black Forest King, had heard their pleas and had granted the supernaturals sanctuary on Enchanted Island as long as they followed certain rules—one of those rules being no admittance onto the north side of the island.

The north side was for Dad's special friends. It was where Randor—a real-life dragon over a thousand years old—like to hide out in his many caves. I also knew it was where a golem named Alfisol—Al for short—made his home. Even Kraken liked to burrow down off the north side as well as the west. It was because of them Dad was constantly using his magic to change the coastline on the north side of the island. He wanted to make sure those who had lived on the island the longest were never disturbed.

I stood and surveyed the surrounding area. "Twenty acres. Where to start?"

"The plant would need access to the moon overhead as well as water," Needles said as he landed on my shoulder. *"So my guess would be we stick near the edge."*

I snorted. "That's still a lot of ground to cover."

A sudden ripple in the water caught my attention. Seconds later, a tiny head poked through the surface. Catching sight of me, the otter flipped over on his back and waved.

"Hello! It sure is busy around here lately. Will you play with me? No one ever wants to play."

"Hello, Mr. Otter. My name is Shayla. Black Forest King is my dad."

The otter righted himself in the water and clapped his paws. *"Have you come to play, Princess?"*

Needles shot up off my shoulder, his wings glowing red and gold. *"The princess does not play. We are here for a purpose, Otter."*

The excitement fell from the otter's young face, and he stopped clapping. *"Oh. No one ever wants to play."*

I smiled and knelt back down, running my hand across the surface of the water and sending a cluster of lily pads slithering away. "What's your name?"

"Olly."

"Well, Olly, what games do you like to play?"

The otter dipped below the surface and then popped up in front of me. *"Hide and seek is my favorite! I played last night with a frog."* He flipped over on his back, grinning. *"I hid so good, he never found me. I hid almost the entire night! I finally had to come out and show him where I was. He was sittin' on his lily pad, and he said he was just thinkin' about where I was hiding."*

Needles snorted. *"I think they call that game just plain old hide."*

I gave Needles a pointed look. No sense hurting the little otter's feelings. "Olly, did you notice anyone else out here last night?"

"Sure did." Olly, still on his back, threw out his arms and turned lazily in a circle. *"There was a couple swimming in the water last night. I hid from them too."*

I frowned. "A couple? Was one of them an older witch?"

"Older? Nope. A werewolf and a—" He stopped twirling and sat up. *"I couldn't really tell what she was. After they swam, they kissed!"* He shuddered, flinging water everywhere. *"Gross! Then they got out, and he shifted and ran under the full moon somewhere else. I couldn't see him anymore. She collected moon water from the lagoon. And then he came back, shifted, and they left. Kissing and laughing. Gross!"*

I hid a smile. "So you didn't see an older witch gathering herbs or flowers?"

Olly shook his wet head. *"No. But it's a big lagoon, Princess."*

"That it is." I stood and waved. "We need to get back to work. Enjoy the rest of your day, Olly."

"Bye, Princess! Come back when you want to play!"

When he disappeared under the water, I looked over at Needles. "You go right, and I'll take left?"

Needles shot off my shoulder, saluted, and zipped to the right while I made my way left across the wet jagged rocks and boulders. I'd gone about twenty yards when I noticed something lying on the ground.

Using my magic, I levitated the item in the air, examining the light-weight jacket. There was something vaguely familiar about it. Conjuring a large evidence bag, I levitated the jacket inside. I was about to look around some more when I heard the flutter of Needles' wings over the roar of the waterfall.

"Princess! Come quick! She's dead!"

I knew better than to ask too many questions. Shoving the baggie in my backpack, I took off after Needles, doing my best to keep up with him as I ran across the slippery, moss-covered rocks.

"Just a little farther ahead," Needles called out.

As I jumped over the gnarled roots of a mangrove, I came to a skittering halt. Half in and half out of the water lay the body of an older woman—a witch.

I crept over to where the witch's body lay sprawled along the edge of the freshwater lagoon, trying not to sink along the sandy bank. When I finally neared her body, I conjured a pair of gloves and booties. Slipping them on, I tiptoed over to her. Glancing down, I couldn't help but notice the smooth, bloody Riverstone rock that lay next to her on the ground.

"I'll call it in."

4

"I thought you were covering the north side of the island today?" Alex mused.

"I was."

I quickly filled him and Grant in on what Tommy had told me and how my morning had changed. As I talked, Doc Drago and Finn Faeton arrived on scene.

Grant was not only a detective for the Enchanted Island Sheriff's Department, but he was also married to my cousin, Serena. Doc Drago was the medical examiner, and Finn Faeton, an eclectic fairy, was our forensic scientist.

"I didn't examine her body," I said. "I figured I'd let Doc do that. The only thing I did was scan her right index finger. It's a match for Selma Greenleaf."

"I got something," Doc called out.

Alex, Grant, and I walked over to where Doc and Finn were examining the body and surrounding area.

"Looks like part of a flower," Doc said, pointing to her left hand.

"I saw it," I said, "but I didn't want to remove it until you had a chance to examine her. I saw a couple crushed petals around her as well."

Finn levitated the flower out of Selma's hand until it was eye-level with us. "What *is* this flower? It doesn't look like anything I've ever come across."

I frowned and leaned in closer for a better look. "It's supposed to be a flower from the Lunar Blossom, but I know the Lunar Blossom. This isn't it."

Finn moved her hand, causing the flower to mimic her movements. "Look at the petals. They look…"

"It's a hybrid," I said.

Finn nodded and dropped the flower in an evidence bag. "I would agree. Once I get it to the lab, I can determine what kind of hybrid it is."

"Selma told people she had a couple Lunar Blossom plants," I said. "She obviously lied."

"I'm pretty sure blunt force trauma is our cause of death," Doc said. "I'll make that determination once the autopsy is finished, but the contusion on the side of her head leads me to make that assumption. Also, rigor suggests she's been dead just over twelve hours."

"So sometime after midnight," I murmured.

"Again, I'll know more after the autopsy," Doc said as he stood. "Which I should have for you first thing in the morning."

"Same with forensics," Finn added.

"One more thing," Doc said. "I found this in the pocket of her dress."

He handed Alex a business card with his gloved hand.

"Hannah Trueheart," Alex read.

"I know Hannah," Finn said. "She recently opened a spa on the south side of the island."

"That's what the business card says," Alex agreed.

Needles zipped over to where we all stood. *"I've spoken to a couple deer. They were foraging in the forest last night, but they didn't see anyone near the lagoon."*

"I found this jacket." I pulled the evidence bag from my backpack. "It wasn't near here, though. It was a little farther down the embankment."

"That belongs to Dash," Grant said, taking the bag from me.

Dash Stryker was a werewolf shifter who owned a construction company on the island. He and Grant often ran together during the full moon. I'd met Dash, and his younger brother, when I first returned to the island a few years back. They were both suspects in the murder investigation I'd been helping Alex with. Dash was currently dating Devona Flame, a normal from a witch family.

"I thought the jacket looked familiar," I said. "I just couldn't place it."

"Surely you don't think Dash did this?" Grant mused.

I shook my head. "Nope. Like I said, the jacket was found a distance from here, but Dash might know something. An otter told me he saw a werewolf and a woman out here last night."

"Dash was probably running under the full moon," Grant said. "I know Devona is still practicing her magic."

Even though Devona was a normal—someone born into a supernatural family, but had no abilities of their own—she still insisted on trying to hone her witch powers. She'd even enlisted the help of another powerful witch on the island, Hagatha Broomly, to help her.

Alex crossed his arms over his chest. "So we have a dead body, a murder weapon left at the scene, a flower that probably isn't the Lunar Blossom, a spa owner's calling card, and a jacket belonging to Dash."

"Do you want me to talk with Dash?" Grant asked.

I shook my head. "No. I better do it." I smiled. "I'd like to see Devona as well."

"No way either one of them killed the old witch," Grant said.

"I know," I agreed. "But I have to follow the clues."

Alex kissed my temple. "I assume you're taking the lead?"

"Darn right we are, Gargoyle. The body was found half in the lagoon. That's our territory."

I gave Alex my most charming smile. "Needles is right. I feel this falls under the jurisdiction of fish and wildlife."

Alex sighed. "Do you have any suspects Grant and I can run for you?"

"Tommy gave me Donald Frasier's name," I said. "Plus, I've spoken to the granddaughter, Ella Greenleaf."

"I didn't like her. I say we haul her in and put the screws to her."

Alex snorted. "You always want to put the screws to someone."

"I have to agree with Needles," I said. "She gave off a lot of red-flag warnings. But she also gave me Regina Hawthorn's name. And now, with the business card found in Selma's pocket belonging to Hannah Trueheart, that brings my list of possible suspects to four."

❀   *5*   ❀

An hour later, with the scene processed and the body of Selma Greenleaf with Doc and Finn on the way back to the lab, Alex, Grant, Needles, and I decided to call it a day. There was no trace of the hybrid plant's home anywhere along the lagoon's edge.

"Could you two do me a favor?" I asked Grant and Alex. "I'm going to tell Ella about her grandmother, but I was wondering if you could get a warrant and go to Selma's house and take a look around there? See if maybe she had notes on this hybrid plant she was trying to pass off as a Lunar Blossom, or anything else you can find that might be helpful to the investigation?"

"We can do that for you," Alex said.

We were almost to our vehicles when Dash and Devona burst through the overgrown foliage—both laughing and hanging on to each other.

"Oh!" Devona cried, stopping in her tracks and pressing a hand to her chest. "What are you guys doing out here?"

I smiled. "I could say the same to you two. Playing hooky from work today?"

Devona giggled and rested her head against Dash's shoulder. "Something like that. We had a few errands to run this morning, and then we decided to just spend the day together instead of at our jobs. Plus, Dash forgot something out here last night. "

Devona was a blogger and freelance writer for a couple different witch magazines. She once joked she educated and informed other witches how to do the one thing she could not—perform spells and mix potions.

"So you both were out here last night?" I asked.

"Yep." Devona looked up at Dash, and I didn't miss the heated look that passed between them.

"What time was that?" Alex asked.

"What?" Dash asked, still gazing down at Devona.

Grant cleared his throat. "Dash? We need to ask you some questions."

Dash pulled his gaze away from Devona. "Yeah, man. What's up?" He must have caught the seriousness on Grant's face because he pulled Devona close. "What's going on?"

"What time were you out here last night?" Alex repeated.

Dash shrugged and looked at Devona. "It was late. I'd say maybe 10:00 or 10:30 when we arrived. We stayed a couple hours."

"I love coming out here and collecting moon water on full moon nights," Devona said. "Why? Is this area off limits? I wasn't aware."

I shook my head. "No. Nothing like that."

"So you got here around 10:00 or 10:30?" Alex prompted. "Then what?"

"Devona and I went for a swim," Dash said. "And then I went for a run from about 11:30 until 12:30, give or take."

"And then you two left?" I asked.

Dash and Devona glanced down at each other, both blushing and grinning.

"Well, not exactly," Dash said.

"If this story ends with them being naked, I'm cutting off my ears," Needles said, whipping out a quill from his back.

"Is Needles okay?" Devona asked, pulling out of Dash's embrace. "Why did he yank out one of his quills?"

Not wanting to embarrass either of them, I hurried on with my questioning. "So what time would you say you left?"

"Maybe around 1:00 or 1:15." Dash frowned. "Are you sure everything is okay?"

"Did you hear anything last night?" Grant asked, ignoring Dash's question.

"Hear anything?" Dash mused. "No."

"What exactly do you mean?" Devona asked.

"Maybe hear arguing or yelling?" I suggested.

Devona frowned. "Maybe. I thought it was just a bird. Or, at least, that's what I told myself."

Dash glanced down at Devona. "You heard something while I was gone? Why didn't you tell me when I returned from my run?"

"I thought it was all in my head. You know, I'm out here all alone while you're running. I thought maybe I heard something, but then I just assumed it was my imagination running away from me."

"What do you think you heard?" Alex asked.

"I thought someone yelled out, 'It's mine!' And then I thought I heard a scream. But, again, by that time, I was convinced I was just freaking myself out."

I nodded. "Okay. How long would you say it was from the time you heard the scream until Dash returned?"

27

"I don't know. Maybe fifteen minutes?" She gave a small laugh. "After I convinced myself it was just my imagination, I went back to focusing on gathering moon water and putting it in jars until Dash returned."

"Are you making more tea?" I mused. "I still remember the last time you served me moon-water tea. It was a blend you made yourself, and it was delicious."

Devona bit her lip and looked up at Dash. "Should we tell them?"

Dash grinned. "Yep. Although it's still a secret."

"I was gathering moon water to make a fertility tea." Devona jumped up and down. "Dash asked me to marry him last night, and we want to start a family as soon as possible!"

"That's great, man!" Grant slapped Dash on the shoulder, then drew him close for one of those hearty man-hug beatdowns.

Devona threw her arms around me, knocking Needles off my shoulder.

"Oops," she giggled, stepping back from me. "Sorry, Needles. I was just excited."

"If it were for any other reason, I'd be insulted." He bowed, his wings glowing silver and gold. *"But a wedding is a joyous occasion."*

"He says congrats," I said.

Dash shook Alex's hand. "Thanks. We both agree we don't want a long, drawn-out engagement."

"That's right," Devona agreed. "So we've invited Hagatha Broomly over for a late supper and spring equinox celebration tomorrow night. We're going to ask her to marry us in April."

"Wow," I said. "That *is* fast."

Devona smiled. "It's going to be a small ceremony. I've already spoken to my sister, and she's agreed to fly in, and, of course, our parents are thrilled. That's where we were this morning." The smile fell from her face. "I dragged my feet for so long. I was afraid of what others might think when it became public knowledge Dash was marrying a normal. I was afraid."

Dash scowled. "I don't care about any of that."

"I know," Devona whispered, her eyes meeting mine. "I know it sounds silly, but I was hoping the full moon water might help make sure any future babies would be shifters as well, or even have a little witch magic in them."

My heart twinged at Devona's honest statement. "If you believe it will help, then do it. Intention is everything."

"Thanks." She smiled again. "And even if our children won't have any supernatural qualities about them, it won't matter to us."

I couldn't help but think Devona was trying to convince *herself* more than us. "Well, I'm sure Hagatha will be thrilled to marry you. So she doesn't know yet?"

Devona shook her head. "Nope. We're going to tell her together tomorrow night. Right now, only our parents, my sister, and now you guys know."

"I hate to break this good news up," Alex said, "but we need to ask a couple more questions."

"What's really going on?" Dash asked. "I can tell there's something wrong."

"Only if you consider the murder of a greedy witch wrong," Needles quipped.

I cleared my throat and glared over at Needles before turning back to Dash and Devona. "Do either of you know Selma Greenleaf?"

"I don't," Dash said.

"I do. Well, sort of. I know her name, but I don't know her personally. She wasn't one of the witches Hagatha warned me to stay away from."

"Hagatha warned you away from witches?" I mused. "Can you tell me names?"

Devona shrugged. "Sure. I don't see why not. She said there were three witches on the island who were unethical. Cedelia Cornrow, Regina Hawthorn, and Maggie Rivers."

"She said Regina Hawthorn?" I mused. "I'd agree with that. I don't know the other two witches. What did she say about Regina?"

Devona winced and shook her head. "I'm sorry. I don't know the full story about Regina because I'm not privy to coven matters, but Hagatha said she was kicked out of her coven a few years back. I'm sure you can ask your mom or GiGi about it. Hagatha just said Regina was asked to leave whatever coven she was in, and I shouldn't have any dealings with her."

I nodded. "I'll be sure and ask Mom or GiGi about her." I cleared my throat. "I just discovered Selma Greenleaf's body not far from here. She'd been murdered."

"Oh, that's awful!" Devona exclaimed.

"Near here?" Dash demanded. "You're thinking she was murdered last night?"

Devona grabbed hold of Dash's arm. "So I really *did* hear someone scream?"

"It's possible," Grant said. "That's why we need to ask these questions."

"Of course," Dash said. "I just can't believe…"

I knew Dash was thinking of his younger brother and of the murders he'd committed just a few years before.

"Hey." Devona reached up and ran her hand over Dash's face. "You okay?"

"Yeah," Dash whispered.

But I could see he wasn't.

"He looks like he's about to keel over," Needles said.

30

"You want to talk," Grant said, "you know how to get ahold of me."

That simple statement seemed to pull Dash from his personal nightmare. He nodded and gave Grant a small smile. "Thanks, man. You're a good friend."

"Listen, Dash," I said. "Needles and I found your jacket. I'm afraid it's been confiscated. Finn took it back to the lab."

"No problem." He drew Devona close again. "What about us? I mean, I don't worry about me, but what about Devona?"

"What about me?" Devona asked.

He glanced down at her before looking at Grant. "Do you think the person who killed Selma Greenleaf knows Devona was out here last night? Do you think they'll try to—"

"No!" Devona slapped her hand across Dash's mouth. "Don't even put that out in the universe."

I was pretty sure Devona still suffered from PTS. GiGi, Needles, and I had been the ones who'd discovered her body in her backyard years ago on my first case. Dash's brother had savagely attacked her with a knife and left her for dead. It had taken all three of us just to keep her alive until the paramedics reached her.

Dash gently lowered her hand. "I want to make sure you're protected."

"I'm sure there's nothing to worry about," Alex said. "But if it makes you feel better, Grant and I can patrol past her house during the day."

Dash and Devona looked at each other and nodded.

"I'd appreciate that," Devona whispered. "Dash usually comes over in the evenings, but during the day, knowing you'll both be patrolling will bring me peace of mind."

❦ 6 ❧

*"*W*ant to take bets on her reaction?"* Needles mused as I opened the front door to Teas, Tinctures, & Tonics.

The witches' bells once again rang out, announcing our arrival. This time, Ella was positioned behind the counter, leafing through a magazine.

"Did you find her home?" Ella demanded, tossing the magazine aside. "What did she say? Why haven't I heard from her yet? Were there others there at the house?"

I glanced over at the tonics area where the old witch was still sitting behind the counter, sleeping the afternoon away.

"We need to talk," I said to Ella. "I'm afraid I have bad news."

Ella gasped. "Bad news? She already sold the Lunar Blossom, didn't she?" She hopped down off the barstool she'd been perched on behind the counter. "I knew it! She never had any intention of letting me bid for the plant!" She slammed her hands down on the counter, causing the elderly witch to let out a loud snore. "She won't get away with it!"

"Ella," I snapped. "You need to calm down and listen to me. Do you know where your grandmother went last night to harvest the plants?"

"Yes. Luna Lagoon. That's where the moon kisses the water. Duh! Why?"

"I drove out there to look around before going to see your grandmother. I'm afraid I found your grandmother's body out there. She'd dead, Ella. I'm very sorry for your loss."

For a few seconds, Ella said nothing. "What about the Lunar Blossom? Did you find it?"

"Did you hear what I just said?" I demanded. "I found your grandmother's body out at Luna Lagoon. She's dead."

"I heard you. And I'm all broken up about it. Honest, I am. But I'm pretty sure Granny would want me to have the Lunar Blossom, if you found it."

"Reason 10,560 why I'll never have children."

I pressed my lips together to keep from smiling. "We didn't find where she was harvesting the supposed Lunar Blossom."

"Well, I have no idea where her hideout is. That lagoon is huge. It could be anywhere."

"I need to ask you some questions," I said. "Where were you last night from nine until six this morning?"

Ella reached out and closed the magazine on the counter, not looking me in the eye. "I was gathering special ingredients for my teas that only come out under the full moon. I picked some lunar lavender, nightshade berries, and celestial sage. They can all be found on the northwest side of the island."

I crossed my arms over my chest, and Needles struck the same pose. Or at least he tried to. He was a little too round in the belly for his arms to across his body.

"How about we try that again," he grumbled, his wings glowing red and black.

"Let's try to be a little more specific with our answers, okay?" I said. "Where were you from nine o'clock until six o'clock?"

Ella huffed. "It's not like I killed my grandma, so I don't see why it matters." She threw up her hands. "But whatever. I went to Boos & Brews and had a couple drinks."

"What time did you leave there?"

"I don't know. It was before midnight because I left the bar and drove to the northwest side of the island to do my gathering." She motioned to a jar sitting on the edge of her counter. "I have yet to put the lunar lavender in my sleepy-time tea, but the other ingredients got shelved today."

"What time did you finish gathering?" I asked.

"Maybe 1:00 or 1:30. After that, I drove home."

"Anyone at home to corroborate that?" I asked.

"I told you this morning I didn't see my grandma, so no. There's no one."

"No familiar or other animal?" I mused.

Ella scoffed. "I don't have time for that. This stupid shop keeps me working all hours of the day." She stuck out her bottom lip. "I thought having a shop would be fun. It's not. It's a lot harder than I bargained for."

"How do you think your grandmother got to the lagoon?" I asked. "We didn't see a car anywhere near the lagoon."

"She rides this bright yellow moped. You didn't see it?"

I shook my head. "It could be she stashed it in the foliage somewhere, and we just didn't come across it. I'll go back out and look again later."

"What about her cell phone?" Ella asked. "Did you find it? Maybe she took pictures of where the plant is located out at the lagoon. I think, technically, I'm entitled to the phone."

Needles scoffed. *"Nice try."*

"We didn't find a cell phone," I said. "And even if we did, it would be in evidence. You have no right to it." I rested my hands on the counter and leaned in close. "You know what I find odd? You haven't asked how your grandmother died."

Ella snorted. "I assume someone killed her. I doubt I was the only one angry she was making us bid on the Lunar Blossom. Find out who else she was stringing along, and I'm sure you'll find your killer."

"Or maybe I'm staring at her," Needles grumbled.

I pushed off the counter. "That's all I have for now. Again, I'm sorry about your loss."

"If you find the Lunar Blossom, will I get it? I'm technically her next of kin since my mom died."

I shook my head. "No. When I discover what it was your grandmother was harvesting, there are several tests I'll need to run before I can determine what happens next."

"That's *so* unfair," Ella whined.

"Let's go, Princess, before I give in to impulse and remove her vocal chords."

lex called when Needles and I returned to the Bronco. He and Grant were getting ready to enter the Greenleaf house to look for clues, and he promised to call if they found anything important.

Deciding I needed more info on Selma Greenleaf and Regina Hawthorn, I put in a call to GiGi. If anyone had gossip about those two, it would be GiGi.

"I'm at the houseboat," my grandmother said. "Your mom and Aunt Starla are here. We're deciding on the final menu for tomorrow night's dinner out at Black Forest. Come out here and have a late lunch."

GiGi and her boyfriend, Byron Sealy, had moved into a houseboat on the south side of the island a while back. When I reached the houseboat, I parked near the dock, and Needles settled on my shoulder as I strolled to the front door. Before I could knock, the door swung open, and Mom yanked me in for a hug.

"I haven't seen you in days," she scolded. "Your dad told me yesterday he hadn't seen you, either."

"I've been a little busy," I said. "I plan on going to Black Forest tonight to see him."

"Good." Mom dragged me through the living room and into the kitchen where GiGi, Aunt Starla, and the twins were hanging out.

"Hey, Brooke. Hey, Cayden." I waved to Serena's seven-month-old twins playing on the floor. "Are you behaving?"

In response, the twins looked up at me, a devilish twinkle in their eyes, and together they levitated their lunch in the air and sent it flying my way.

Laughing, I ducked down...unfortunately, Needles wasn't paying as much attention. He got smacked in the face and body with two hotdogs, which sent him flying backward. The twins giggled and clapped their hands in glee.

"Reason 10,561 why I'm not having kids," Needles grumbled as he shoved the salty dogs in his mouth.

I waggled my finger at the twins before turning to GiGi. "I'm working a case and need your help."

"I'm all ears," she said, stepping back from the spinach burger she was patting.

"I went out to Luna Lagoon today and found Selma Green-leaf's body. She's been murdered."

Aunt Starla and Mom gasped.

"How?" Aunt Starla asked.

"It looks like someone smashed her upside the head with a rock." I glanced over at the twins, hoping they couldn't decipher what I was saying. "I need to know what you can tell me about Selma Greenleaf and Regina Hawthorn."

GiGi snorted. "Both are trouble. No respect for nature or their craft."

I nodded. "That's what I figured. I ran into Devona Flame, and she said Hagatha Broomly warned her away from Regina. So I thought I'd see what you had to say."

After GiGi finished giving me the lowdown on the latest gossip involving both witches, Mom cut a piece of the goat cheese tart, plated it, and slid it over to me. "We're thinking of this tart, the spinach burgers, and a lovely fruit salad."

I took a bite of the tart and moaned. "It's delicious. Perfect for a spring equinox dinner." I wolfed down the rest of the tart, wiped my mouth, and pushed the plate aside. "Selma Greenleaf claimed to have found the Lunar Blossom and was cultivating it and selling it off to the highest bidder."

"The Lunar Blossom?" Aunt Starla mused. "I didn't think the island had but one? And it was on the north side."

"Exactly," I said. "In her left hand, she was clutching what I assumed she was trying to pass off as the Lunar Blossom. Have you ever seen anything like this?" I pulled out my cell phone and passed my phone around.

"Looks like a hybrid," GiGi said.

I nodded. "That's what Finn and I thought as well. She's got it back at her lab trying to figure out the flower's makeup as we speak."

Mom frowned down at my screen. "It looks like a cross between a Moonflower and a Night-Blooming Jasmine."

I heard the telltale sound of Needles snoring and glanced over my shoulder. Sure enough, the little porcupine was nestled between the twins, fast asleep.

"Both are medicinal flowers with beauty and health benefits," Mom added.

"You got any other suspects besides Regina?" GiGi asked.

"A couple. Her granddaughter, for starters. Something about that girl rubs me wrong."

"I heard she opened a tea shop," Aunt Starla said. "I haven't been in yet."

"Anyone else a suspect?" Mom asked.

"Tommy Trollman is the one who alerted me to the whole plant scam," I said. "He gave me Donald Frasier's name. Seems his bar is in trouble, and by getting his hands on the Lunar Blossom, it could save him big money. Last possible suspect I have is Hannah Trueheart. She recently opened a spa. I still have yet to talk to Regina, Donald, and Hannah. I came out here first to get your guys' thoughts."

GiGi laughed. "You ain't fooling no one. You came out here to get fed."

I grinned. "Guilty."

"So you haven't been out to the new spa yet?" Aunt Starla asked.

"Nope. But I'm hoping to go later today."

Aunt Starla beamed. "Maybe you can go after Serena closes the bakery and you can take her with you? She's been working so hard lately. She really deserves a little pampering."

"Sure," I said. "I don't see why not. I'll call and see what I can set up."

Mom finished the last of her tart. "I'll take the twins with me when I go home and keep them at Serena and Grant's place until they get home."

"Thank you, Serenity," Aunt Starla said. "That's very kind of you."

As if knowing we were talking about them, the twins broke out into a babble only they understood. Lifting their hands in the air, they levitated Needles off the ground. Praying he wouldn't wake up and have a heart attack, I turned back around and did my best to ignore their adorable antics.

"So," Mom said, clasping her hands together, "what should we serve for dinner tomorrow night?"

"Definitely the goat cheese tart," I said.

"What's going on?" Needles demanded. *"Why am I upside down and touching the ceiling?"*

I glanced over my shoulder again and burst out laughing at the sight of Needles floating upside down, his back paws touching the ceiling. "Let me guess? This is reason 10,562?"

"Darn right, it is. Now, stop this levitation nonsense and get me down from here, Princess!"

❧ 8 ❧

On my way out to Regina Hawthorn's place on the west side of the island, I placed a call to Hannah Trueheart's spa, Tranquil Tides. Luck was with me when she answered the phone herself.

"Hannah? My name is Shayla Loci-Stone. I'm the game warden for Enchanted Island. I was hoping to speak to you sometime today. It's urgent."

"The game warden? Is something wrong?"

"Just a couple questions I need to ask you," I said. "Can you squeeze me in?"

"I have some time around 3:30 today."

"Perfect." I paused, not sure how to ask the next part without sounding like I wanted an out-right favor. "I don't suppose you'd have time to do a facial and massage for me and my cousin, would you?"

"Oh, let me check the calendar here."

Needles cleared his throat and gave me a pointed look.

"Uh, this may sound odd, but my partner, Needles, would

also like to be pampered as well. He's a miniature porcupine. Would that be possible?"

There was a moment of silence before Hannah spoke. "Sure. I guess so. We've never worked on a porcupine before."

"Don't worry. I'll spell his quills to be soft and supple."

"Umm…okay. I have three for facials and massages at 3:30 today. Is that correct?"

"Sounds great. See you then." I disconnected and called Serena as I turned left onto the gravel road where Regina Hawthorn lived. "Did you ride in with Grant this morning?"

"Yes," Serena said. "And Mom has already called me and said I'm to go with you for spa pampering, and that Aunt Serenity will watch the twins at our cottage until Grant gets home."

"Good. I'll pick you up at the bakery a little after 3:00."

Disconnecting one last time, I turned onto a gravel driveway. Regina's cottage was partially hidden behind tall shrubs and hedges. I parked and got out of the Bronco and proceeded to the front door with Needles on my shoulder…until I heard music at the back of the house. Pivoting, I turned and made my way around back.

Regina Hawthorn was standing on her enclosed back deck, listening to music as she stirred something in her cauldron. Without missing a beat, she looked up and smiled.

"Well, hello Shayla. Long time, no see." She waved her left hand over the cauldron—using her magic to continue stirring—and motioned for me to come closer. "I was about to put on the kettle. Care for some hot tea?"

"No, thank you." I opened the screen door and stepped inside. "I just need to ask you a couple questions."

"Of course. I suppose this is about that ridiculous notion of Selma Greenleaf having the Lunar Blossom?"

I blinked in surprise. I hadn't expected her to outright admit she knew about the flower. "Yes, it is."

Regina waved her left hand in the air. "You needn't worry. I already know it's a fake. A hybrid."

"How do you know?" I asked.

"Because she saw it last night when she killed Selma," Needles said in my ear.

"I went to see Selma last night. I wanted to see this supposed Lunar Blossom for myself. When she finally relented and showed me a picture on her phone, I realized immediately it was a fake. I told her to take me off her list of contacts. I was no longer interested."

"So you knew it was a fake?"

Regina let out a bark of laughter. "Please! You don't think I'm smart enough to know a hybrid flower when I see one?" Regina shook her head, her chin-length hair moving with her. "I told her to pawn off that garbage to other unsuspecting buyers. I wasn't biting."

"And this was last night?" I mused.

"Yes. I drove out to see her." She waved a hand dismissively in the air. "Well, I was already in town having grabbed dinner at the Enchanted Island Café. But afterward, I went to see Selma."

"What time was that?"

"I don't know. Maybe 7:00 or 7:15? Somewhere around there. Why?"

"Just trying to get a feel for the timeline is all."

Regina frowned. "Did Selma call you to complain?" She rolled her eyes. "That's pretty bold of her, don't you think? She supposedly acquires one of the most elusive plants in the world, and *she's* filing a complaint against me? Maybe you should question her about why she's trying to pass off an obvious fake to other supernaturals."

"I would," I said, watching her carefully, "but she's dead. I discovered her body out at Luna Lagoon earlier today."

Regina's eyes went wide, but she recovered quickly. "Really? Well, I can't say I'm surprised. I'm probably not the only one who realized she was trying to pull a fast one. Trust me, if I was suspicious, I'm sure whoever else she approached was suspicious as well."

"I want her to be guilty because she's unethical, but it could be she's right, Princess."

I'd already considered that, of course. "So she approached you? Tell me about that."

"Two weeks ago, give or take, she rode her moped out to my place. She said she had discovered the Lunar Blossom a while back while foraging. And it wasn't just one plant, but many. She said the first plant would be ready after the full moon—which was last night. All she needed from me was commitment I'd bid on the plant. And before you frown and look at me all disapprovingly, just know I don't care. It's not illegal to obtain a Lunar Blossom, so, of course, I wanted it."

"But something happened to change your mind?"

"The more I thought about it, the more I realized it probably wasn't real. Or maybe Selma *thought* it was authentic, but there's no way, right? So before I plunked down a substantial amount of money, I wanted to see it with my own eyes. That's why I went to see her last night. I wanted proof."

"And she showed you a picture? On her cell phone?"

"The cell phone that's missing," Needles pointed out.

"Yep, on her cell phone. And I knew immediately it couldn't be the Lunar Blossom. Granted, I don't know *exactly* what it looks like, but I found it hard to believe it would look like a hybrid of two species I recognized, and one I didn't."

I nodded. "So you recognized the flowers she used to make the hybrid plant?"

Regina nodded. "I recognized two of the flowers. I can't say for sure, but I *think* there might be something else besides the two flowers I recognized." She shrugged. "But that's just a guess."

"Did she ever tell you where the plants were planted?"

Regina shook her head. "Nope. Just that they'd be ready to cultivate on the night of the full moon."

"Where did you go after your altercation last night with Selma?"

"I drove out to the south side of the island to gather petals from the night-bloom flower and a handful of moon mushrooms." She pointed to the cauldron. "That's what I'm making now—a dream tea. It's supposed to help with prophetic dreams."

"What time did you get home last night?" I asked.

"Not sure. It was before midnight."

"Were you alone?"

"Completely."

9

"What do you think?" I asked Needles as we pulled out of Regina's gravel drive.

"She said all the right things, but she can't be trusted. You gave her a citation for unauthorized harvesting of magical herbs. If she's done it once, she'd do it again."

"You think she followed Selma out to the lagoon, confronted her, killed her, and then took the hybrids for herself?"

"It's a theory."

My cell phone rang, and I picked it up. "Whaddya got for me?"

"We found a list of potential buyers," Alex said. "The four names you've already mentioned are on here, plus about three others. Two of those three were crossed off, which Grant and I took to mean they were a no when confronted, but that still leaves one more name."

"Who is it?" I asked.

"Marvina Darkstone."

I frowned. "That name sounds familiar."

"Vampire," Needles said from the backseat.

"I looked her up on the app," Alex said. "She lives about five miles north of town." He rattled off the address. "Do you want to take her, or do you want Grant and me to question her?"

"I'm in the Bronco right now heading back into town. I can make a quick stop."

"That's all we found," Alex said.

"No cell phone?"

"Nope. No cell phone."

"Okay. Can you check with the crossed-off names and question them? See if Selma approached them and make sure they're a no?"

"Can do," Alex said.

I disconnected and turned right at the next major road that would take me north of town where Marvina Darkstone lived. In less than ten minutes, I pulled into the driveway and parked in front of a black, two-story Gothic-style home, complete with towering spires and pointed arches. I unlocked the heavy, wrought-iron gate and strode across the cobblestone walkway up to the front door.

"This looks like a sunny little place to live," Needles joked.

Grinning, I lifted the bat doorknocker and gave it a couple raps. Seconds later, a harried-looking witch I guessed to be in her mid-twenties with long brown hair pulled into a messy ponytail stood in the doorway. She looked like she hadn't slept in days if the dark smudges and heavy bags under her green eyes were to be believed. She was dressed in a brown sweater and brown pants. She didn't smile—just simply stared.

"Hello," I said. "My name is Agent Loci-Stone, and I'm the game warden for Enchanted Island."

"Hazel Birchwood," she said.

"I need to speak to Marvina Darkstone."

The disheveled witch shook her head, her dark hair seeming to take on a life of its own. "No can do. Ms. Darkstone is busy creating her next masterpiece."

Needles' wings fluttered wildly next to my ear.

I gave her a small smile. "I'm afraid I must insist, Hazel. It's a law enforcement matter."

The young woman looked uncertainly over her shoulder, as if unsure what to do.

"It's important," I said.

Sighing, Hazel Birchwood stepped back and motioned us inside. "Okay. But you can't stay long. I'll tell her you're here and make her favorite drink. That should soothe her."

I stepped inside the foyer and was immediately assaulted with the faintest hints of patchouli and sandalwood. The dark hardwood floor seemed dull and lifeless under the glow of the one lonely candle floating above us. The wooden staircase loomed to the right of the room and six Gothic-inspired paintings encased in hand-carved ornate wooden frames lined the wall, heading upstairs.

"Marvina Darkstone," I whispered. "Now I know why her name sounded familiar."

"Ms. Darkstone is known worldwide in the supernatural art world." Hazel Birchwood led us down a narrow hallway before stopping in front of an arched doorway. "Please give me a minute to rouse Ms. Darkstone. She's in a—well, she's not feeling herself today."

Needles and I stood in the doorway as Hazel sighed and stepped inside the nearly pitch-black room. All the heavy drapes were pulled shut, with not a single ray of light peeking inside. The flickering glow of the fire in the fireplace was the only light in the room.

"Ms. Darkstone," Hazel said softly. "There's someone here to see you."

In an instant, the body that had been lying supine on the velvet-covered chaise lounge sat up. "Is it her? Is it the old witch with my Lunar Blossom?"

Hazel cleared her throat and cast a quick, furtive look my way before shaking her head. "No, ma'am. It's an Agent Loci-Stone. She needs to speak to you. "

The vampire shot up a bandaged hand, narrowly missing the young woman's face. "Send her away! I can't see anyone today." She dropped back down on the chaise, one arm now thrown over her eyes. "I need my creative juice, Hazel!"

"I know, Ms. Darkstone." She stood and cleared her throat. "I'm going to go make your favorite drink. Do you think you could please just try to listen to what the woman has to say? I promise to be right back with your drink."

"Fine," the vampire whined. "But only for a minute. And hurry with my drink. I have a deadline looming, and I have no creativity!"

The last was said on a wail, and I nearly winced at the eardrum-splitting sound.

Hazel gave me a tight smile before hurrying out of the room. When the vampire didn't ask me to enter or even attempt to move, I sighed and strode inside the dark room.

"She screams killer to me, Princess. Watch yourself."

I stepped over to the fireplace and leaned against the mantle. "Ms. Darkstone, I'm Agent Loci-Stone. I need to ask you some questions about Selma Greenleaf. Do you know her?"

At the sound of Selma's name, the vampire sat up again and gasped. "Yes! Did she send you with my Lunar Blossom?" In the blink of an eye, the vampire rose and stood a few inches from me. "Where is it? Give it to me!"

"Step back, Vampire." Needles hovered between us, his wings glowing red and two quills in his paws. *"I won't lose any sleep gutting you."*

"I don't have the Lunar Blossom," I said. "That's why I'm here. I need to speak to you about it and Selma Greenleaf."

"Why hasn't she called?" Marvina Darkstone ran her hands through her short dark hair, pulling the ends from her head. "Is she demanding more money? Whatever it is, I'll pay." Her eyes glowed red, and I almost took a step backward. "She gave me a sample, you know. Oh, the gloriousness of it!" She zipped over to a canvas on an easel across the room that I hadn't seen in the dark. "Look at this! Isn't it amazing? I did this after one taste of the Lunar Blossom. It's my muse. I must have it!"

I strained my eyes to see the painting, but the room was too dark to make it out. I could use my imagination, though. I'd seen Marvina Darkstone's paintings many times throughout my lifetime.

"I had no idea you lived on Enchanted Island," I said. "Have you lived here long?"

"What?" Marvina scowled. "Why does that matter? Nothing matters but the flower and my art."

"I need you to focus," I said. "Have you lived on the island long?"

Marvina flung a hand in the air. "I don't know. Maybe eight years? Maybe ten? Who knows? Time is irrelevant to a vampire, you silly little witch."

"I suppose it is," I murmured. "How did you hurt your hand, Ms. Darkstone?"

Marvina glanced down at her hand and frowned. "I don't know. I probably cut it while working. I don't remember."

"I'm afraid I have bad news regarding Selma Greenleaf," I said. "She was found murdered earlier today."

For a few seconds, Marvina Darkstone stood so still, I thought maybe she hadn't heard me. Then, in the blink of an eye, she tore through the room in a fit of rage, throwing vases and overturning furniture—screaming at the top of her lungs the entire time.

Hazel Birchwood hurried into the room, a silver chalice clutched tightly in her hand. She took in the chaos happening, turned to me, then glanced back at the whirlwind who was Marvina Darkstone.

"What's going on?" Hazel demanded. "What have you done? What did you say to her?"

"I simply told her Selma Greenleaf is dead," I said, tired of the theatrics. Famous artist or not, Marvina Darkstone was a huge drama queen, and I didn't have time for such nonsense. I had a killer to catch.

Hazel gasped. "Dead? But she promised to call today. She has…" She trailed off and averted her gaze. "Here, Marvina. Take your drink." She handed Marvina the chalice and gently led her to the chaise. "Let's sit down, Marvina. Take a sip of your enhancement drink. It'll help."

"A thousand pretzel rods says there's some kind of drug in that drink."

Because I was sure Needles was right, I didn't take him up on that bet. The only thing I wasn't sure about was whether or not the "enhancement" was legal or illegal.

Once Marvina gulped down half the glass, Hazel turned to me. "What's going on? Selma is dead? How? We just spoke with her last night."

"Tell me about that," I said. "And I want the truth, Hazel. I already know Selma was trying to pass off what she had as the Lunar Blossom."

Hazel frowned. "That's not what it was?"

"No. Did you not see it?"

Hazel shook her head. "No." She patted Marvina's shoulder and stepped closer to Needles and me. "Listen, I know how this looks, but Marvina is an artist, and sometimes the artistic and creative types need a little help getting things out of their head."

"Uh-huh," I said, not really wanting to hear her excuses for why her employer was using enhancements.

Hazel looked back at Marvina. "It's Museleaf. I'm sure you know it's a natural stimulant. There's nothing illegal about Museleaf."

"Tell me about Selma."

"Selma came by two weeks ago and gave Marvina a sample of the Lunar Blossom. It was like a miracle. After she left, Marvina went into her studio and painted three different pieces! It was…amazing. I'd never seen anything like it." She sighed. "Unfortunately, the enhancement wore off a couple days later, and Marvina was back to struggling for her creativity. So when Selma called to tell Marvina she could have as much of the plant she wanted, she just had to pay for it, Marvina said yes. In a good-faith show, Selma came out three days ago and gave Marvina some more of the Lunar Blossom. She said the first plant would be ready to bid on after the full moon. Which is today." Hazel held up her hand. "And before you get angry, the research I've done on the Lunar Blossom says it's a natural stimulant."

"Too bad Marvina wasn't taking the Lunar Blossom."

I shook my head. "So you're telling me Marvina has ingested whatever it is Selma gave her? Not once, but twice?"

"Yes. But nothing but wonderfulness has come from it," Hazel said. "Like I said, Marvina went on to create three amazing paintings. Usually, that would take six months. She did it in less than four days."

"Is your family from Enchanted Island?" I asked.

Hazel blinked in surprise. "Yes. My mom and grandmother both live on the island. My dad's family, the Birchwood side, doesn't live here. My mom met my dad when she was in college. But my mom and grandma were raised on the island. And both are healers and make potions and spells for others here on the island."

"How old are you?"

"Twenty-seven."

"Knowing what you know about the island," I snapped, "why on earth would you let Ms. Darkstone take an unknown substance?"

Hazel's eyes went wide, and she shook her head emphatically...once again, causing her messy ponytail to fly about her head. "It's not like that. I told you, I did the research. Plus, Marvina is gifted. Her art is some of the most beautiful I've ever seen. She just needs a little help letting it out."

"So is Hazel an enabler or a pusher?" Needles demanded.

I was about to find out.

"Do you live here in the house, or do you come and go every day?"

"I live here. It was one of the requirements. Marvina needs constant supervision, as you can see. Her moods are too chaotic for her to be left alone unsupervised."

"How long has she lived on the island?" I asked.

"Almost six years now."

"And how long have you worked for her?"

"Almost five years. She had a PA before me, but it wasn't working out. So Marvina's publicist put out a notice in the *Supernatural Arts Forum*, a weekly internet magazine, asking for applicants. I have an art history degree, but also living here on the island really sold it." She shrugged. "Marvina's publicist hired me immediately."

"Where were you both last night from nine o'clock until six this morning?"

Hazel's hands flew to her chest. "Are we suspects?"

I gave her a tight smile. "Yes. You have admitted Selma approached you both about the 'supposed' Lunar Blossom. You let Selma supply Ms. Darkstone with an unknown substance that makes her 'creative,' Selma demands payment for more enhancement, and now Selma is dead. Yes, you are both persons of interest."

Needles snorted. *"Also known as suspects."*

Hazel frowned. "Are you *sure* what Marvina has been taking *isn't* a Lunar Blossom enhancement?"

I stared Hazel in the eyes. "I'm sure."

Hazel shot a glance at Marvina Darkstone, who was now humming softly to herself as she lay on the couch, totally oblivious to us.

"Don't worry," Hazel said quickly. "She's just going into her head to draw on her creativity. That's what the Museleaf helps her do."

"Does that mean she's stoned or drunk?" Needles mused.

I bit down on my lip to keep from smiling. "I'm waiting, Hazel. Where were you last night from nine o'clock until six o'clock?"

"Last night? Well, Marvina was still feeling creative, so she worked into the early morning hours."

"How early?" I demanded.

"Maybe one or two in the morning."

"And you were with her during this time?" I asked.

"On and off. I tried to leave her alone as much as possible, but when she'd get agitated or confused, I'd come in and talk with her."

"Pump her with more juicy-juice more like it," Needles said.

"So neither one of you left the house at all?" I said.

"No. We were both here."

"If I ask Marvina, will she say the same thing?"

Hazel bit her lip and looked at Marvina. "I don't know. Sometimes she gets confused. She may tell you she was trapped inside her latest painting. She's been known to do that."

I shook my head. "I've always admired Ms. Darkstone's artwork. The dark, bold strokes and Gothic-inspired settings. I had no idea the woman was such a tortured soul."

Hazel turned her sad green eyes to Marvina. "When I first came to work here, I tried to talk to her about her dependency on the natural enhancements. I tried to get her to see she could achieve her work sober. But it was no use. She wasn't having it. I could either keep my job and give her what she needed...or I could leave." She turned back to me. "I believe in her. I see her talent. I couldn't just walk away and let someone who may not care as much as me step in. So I stay and do the best I can. I've learned there are a lot of natural plants that can give Marvina the boost she needs. She's not a drug addict, Agent Loci-Stone. Everything I give her is a natural enhancement."

Ten minutes later, I pulled to a stop in front of the bakery. I was about to go inside when the front door opened and Serena stepped out. After locking the door, and then adding another layer of protection by using her magic to ward the building, she turned and hurried over to my Bronco.

"I've been waiting two hours for this," she said by way of greeting as she climbed inside. "Ever since Mom told me you were taking me to a spa."

I laughed and pulled out onto the street. "You realize I'm going to interview a potential suspect, right?"

"Don't care. All I hear is I'm getting a facial and massage."

"I'm rather excited myself," Needles admitted from the backseat.

Serena turned around. "You're getting a facial and massage as well, Needles?"

"I'm all tingly at the thought of having my quills manipulated."

"Not even going to touch that one," Serena muttered as she turned back around in her seat.

Grinning, I continued toward the south side of the island where Tranquil Tides was located. As I drove, Serena made small talk about the twins and their latest antics and how she was sure they were mellowing out as they got older. Neither Needles nor I said anything about them levitating Needles upside down just a few short hours ago. I found it was sometimes best to let Serena be ignorant of those little rascals' true nature.

Tranquil Tides Spa was located at the base of a winding road overlooking the ocean. The spa's stucco exterior was light blue with white trim. The thatched roof was covered in moonbeam grass, which meant it would glow silver at night. Luminescent stones lined the pathway to the front door as we strolled through the fragrant, lush garden. The natural sound of the ocean— roaring waves and the call of birds—was the only music needed.

I opened the door for us to step inside, and the smell of salty ocean air and healing herbs greeted me. Crossing the smooth, warm-toned stones, we headed for the front desk. Overhead, glass orbs floated in the air giving off soft, white light.

"Welcome to Tranquil Tides," the young mermaid behind the counter said. "How may I help you?"

"We have a 3:30 appointment," I said. "I'm also supposed to meet with Hannah Trueheart."

"Of course." The mermaid picked up her cell phone and tapped out a message. "I've let Mrs. Trueheart know you are here. Would you like some ice water or herbal tea?"

"I'd love some herbal tea," Serena said.

"Of course." She turned to Needles and me. "Would you and —um, does your friend drink herbal tea as well?"

"I drink rum, my lovely mermaid," Needles said, his wings glowing purple and green.

"Needles and I are fine," I said. "Thank you, anyway."

"Rum, I say!"

The mermaid smiled. "Of course. If you'd like—"

She broke off when a petite fairy dressed in cream linen pants and a plum sleeveless top with silver open-toed sandals strode into the room.

"Hello," the woman said. "I'm Hannah Trueheart."

I stuck out my hand. "I'm Agent Loci-Stone, and this is my cousin, Serena Wolfe, and my partner, Needles."

Needles waggled his purple and green wings at her as Hannah shook Serena's hand.

"Welcome to Tranquil Tides," Hannah said. "Would it be okay if we put you all in the same room? It's our couple's room?"

"Works for me," I said.

"I have no problem with it," Serena added.

"I'm not sure I'm comfortable exposing my body to you both."

I snorted. "You mean the same body we see every day?"

"Excuse me?" Hannah Trueheart said.

I held up a hand and shook my head. "Sorry. I sometimes forget not everyone can hear Needles. He was just being funny."

"So you say, Princess."

Hannah blinked, her eyes wide. "So he can speak to you, and you can hear him?"

"Long story," I said. "Listen, before we start, can I talk with you privately?"

"Yes. I must admit, I've been curious why you called and asked to see me today."

"Do you want me to take them back to their room, Hannah?" the mermaid asked, handing Serena her herbal tea.

"Yes, Gloria. Thank you. We shouldn't be long."

"I'll let you get this one on your own, Princess."

"It's about Selma Greenleaf," I said when the others had gone. "Do you know who she is?"

Fear flittered in Hannah's eyes. "Yes. She stopped by to see me last week." Hannah held up her hands. "I told her I didn't want what she was selling."

"Can you tell me about her visit?"

Hannah sighed. "It was about a week ago. I'm not sure the exact date, sorry. Days sort of run together when you're running a business."

"That's okay. Rough estimate is fine. So sometime last week?"

Hannah nodded. "Yes. She said she'd done her homework and knew of the four spas on the island, mine was hurting the most. I was a little insulted, to be honest. I haven't been in business long, so of course I'm not doing the business like the other spas. Anyway, I don't know why, but I let her talk. She said she could offer me the 'fountain of youth' if I wanted. Said she had a plant that could make my customers look ten years younger after just one use. I could bottle it and sell it to non-magicals and make tons of money." She chuckled and placed a hand on her throat. "I'm a fairy. I know plants, and I know that's not possible. Then she tells me she got her hands on the Lunar Blossom." She looked me in the eye. "I know what that is. That's the holy grail of beauty plants." Hannah closed her eyes and shook her head. "I'm ashamed to say for a moment, I was tempted." She opened her eyes. "But I wasn't about to risk my new business on something like that. I don't even know if that flower really exists or if it's just some myth fairies and witches have been telling throughout the ages."

I didn't dare tell her it was real, and that I knew where it was located on the island.

"Anyway, I told her thanks, but no thanks. She reached down and grabbed my business card off the counter and said she'd keep it and call me again in a couple days to see if I'd changed my mind. I told her not to bother, but she just shrugged and left."

"And that was the last you heard from her?"

"In person? Yes. She called a few days ago to ask me if I was interested yet, and I told her no."

"I'm here asking these questions because I was out at Luna Lagoon this morning and found the body of Selma Greenleaf."

Hannah gasped and took a step backward. "What? She's dead? How?"

"I'm still waiting on the autopsy report," I said. "I need to ask...where were you last night between 9:00 and 6:00 this morning?"

It took a couple seconds before Hannah spoke. "My husband and I went to visit our oldest son's family last night. They just had a baby a few weeks back, and last night was the first time I was able to get away from the spa at a decent hour."

"How long did you stay?"

"Until about 8:00, I'd say. Afterward, we went to High Seas Bar & Grill to have a celebratory drink—or two—for being first-time grandparents. I think we left around 9:30." She lifted a hand. "And that's it. After that, my husband and I went home. By then, I was too tired to do simple spell work under the full moon, so my husband and I just went to bed."

"What time did you get up?"

"About 6:00. I was driving to the spa this morning by 7:15. I put in long hours still because I'm trying to get the business up and going."

"Okay. I think that's all the questions I have for now."

"I'm truly sorry Selma is dead," Hannah said as she led me

down a dimly lit corridor. "It may have been unethical for her to approach me like that, but I never wished harm on her."

She pushed open a door, and I stepped inside. One light orb floated overhead, the light flickering as though it were a candle. Lavender and tea tree oil permeated the room as Serena lay face-down on a massage table. Needles was floating on an enchanted pillow between the two massage tables, a pink mask covering his face.

"This is the life, Princess!"

Smiling, I strolled over and placed my hands above Needles' head. Whispering a spell to make his quills soft, I stepped back and nodded.

"You're all set. Enjoy, Needles."

A tiny pixie with purple wings flew over to us. "Thank you, Miss. I'll start on the massage now."

Shaking my head in wonder, I watched as the diminutive pixie hovered over Needles' body and began manipulating his back. Needles' low groan was nearly my undoing. Waving my hand in front of me, I erected a short-term screen and quickly undressed before sliding under the blanket on the massage table. When I was comfortable, I dropped the screen and glanced over at Serena—now also covered in the same pink facial as Needles.

"Thank you," she whispered. "You don't know how badly I needed this."

Remembering the mischief the twins had gotten into in the brief time I'd been around them, I smiled. "I think maybe I do."

Serena called Grant after we left Tranquil Tides to make sure he was home. Not only was he home, but he and Mom were currently feeding the twins dinner. Serena informed him we had one more stop to make, and then she'd be home. I'd also informed Grant we'd need to run Hazel Birchwood through the system. I knew he already had Marvina on his list, but after speaking with Hazel, I wanted to know more about her as well.

"The pretzels wore off hours ago, Princess," Needles whined from the backseat. *"Let's make this next interview fast."*

I rolled my eyes. "Who's being the princess now?"

Serena let out a bark of laughter. "I've forgotten how much fun it is to ride shotgun with you and Needles. I love my life now that the twins are here, but sometimes I miss our stakeout days."

I pulled into the parking lot of Howling at the Moon and parked. "I must admit, I miss our stakeout days as well."

Donald Frasier's bar, which was located on the east side of the island, wasn't exactly on our way home, but it also wasn't too far out of the way. Once Serena knew the twins were taken care of, she'd eagerly agreed to go with Needles and me for one last interview.

The outside of Howling at the Moon was the epitome of rustic, lupine charm—lots of wood and metal. Even the front door was oversized and engraved with moons and werewolves. Pulling the door open, the three of us entered the bar. I was a little surprised to see it was empty except for a drunken werewolf shifter passed out in a corner booth. Tommy had told me the bar was struggling, but I hadn't expected it to be so desolate at five o'clock.

Massive wooden beams covered the ceiling, matching the polished dark wood of the floors, and werewolf and moon memorabilia hung on the walls. The bar, a slab of gnarled live oak, was positioned to the right of the door in front of a mirrored back bar lined with booze.

"It's actually quite charming," Serena murmured.

"Whaddya want?" the man behind the counter demanded.

"I stand corrected," Serena said.

Before Needles could whip out a freshly massaged quill, I strode over to the bar. "Are you Donald Frasier?"

"So what if I am?" He looked me up and down. "You a cop or something?"

"Game warden. I'm Agent Loci-Stone."

"Stone? Like the sheriff?"

"Never a good sign when a bad guy recognizes the sheriff's name," Needles said, his wings glowing red and black.

"Yes," I said. "He's my husband."

He grinned. "Yeah? Well, he ain't here, so go try some other bar, sweetheart."

"That's it!" Needles exclaimed, shooting off my shoulder and whipping out two quills. *"You lose an eye or a tongue. Take your pick, Werewolf!"*

"Let's all settle down," I said, trying not to laugh as Donald Frasier's eyes went wide. "Needles, I think Mr. Frasier will behave himself."

Needles whipped the quills in the air for good measure. *"See that you do, Werewolf. Otherwise, I got a quill with your name on it!"*

"This is a nice place you have here," I said. "I like the look."

With one more quick glance at Needles, and then Serena, he finally settled on me. "Yeah? Thanks. Now, are you drinking or not?"

"Not," I said. "I need to ask you a few questions about Selma Greenleaf. Do you know her?"

Donald said nothing, just slapped a bottle of tequila on the counter. "You want answers…you drink."

"I could probably do a shot," Serena said. "I can't remember the last time I did one."

"Your bachelorette party," I said dryly. "And I'm not at all surprised to hear you don't remember doing them."

Grinning, Serena settled down on a barstool.

"For every question you ask," Donald said, "the little witch drinks."

Serena nodded. "Deal."

Needles settled down on top of the bar. *"Oh, boy. You're gonna be levitating her into the house, Princess. You know that, right?"*

Clapping her hands in glee, Serena looked expectantly at me as Donald poured the first shot.

"You asked if I knew Selma Greenleaf. That's a shot." He set the tiny glass in front of Serena and waited for her to toss it back. "Yes, I know her." He narrowed his eyes at Serena. "You one of those weak witches who needs salt and lime to choke it down?"

Serena smacked her lips and smiled. "Nope. Next question, Shayla."

Biting my lip to keep from laughing, I asked my next question. "Why did Selma contact you?"

Scowling, Donald poured another drink and passed it to Serena. "I don't know how she knew, but the old witch said she had it on good authority my business was struggling. She said she had an offer for me. So if you're here to tell me that just listening to her offer was illegal, you're wrong. I know my rights."

"I'm sure he does."

Serena tossed back the tequila and slammed the glass on the counter.

"You doing okay?" I mused.

"Right at rain...drops keep falling on my head." She threw back her head and laughed. "Get it?"

I rolled my eyes. "Oh, boy. Grant is going to kill me. Okay, Mr. Frasier, next question. What did Selma try to sell you?"

A strange look passed over Donald Frasier's face. "Something that would solve all my problems. Only thing is, she obviously lied."

"Don't you dare drink that," I said to Serena. "He hasn't answered my question yet."

Serena sighed. "Well, get on with it, man!"

"What did she try to sell you?" I repeated.

Donald Frasier scowled and crossed his arms over his massive chest. "The Lunar Blossom. When used in combination with booze, it makes the alcohol three times more potent than it should be."

I nodded. "Meaning you can water your drinks down and make the booze go farther?"

"Maybe. Ain't nothing illegal about that."

"Did he answer?" Serena asked.

"He answered," I said.

"Yippie." Serena tossed back the drink, closed her eyes, shook her head, swallowed, and pounded on the bar. "Whoohoo!"

"She's maybe got two more questions in her, Princess. Make them good."

"When's the last time you spoke with Selma Greenleaf?" I asked.

"Yesterday afternoon. She said she'd call me today to bid on the plant." His nostrils flared as he poured another drink for Serena. "She obviously either never had the Lunar Blossom, or she sold it out from under me without giving me a chance to bid on it because I never heard from her today."

"So you were interested in buying it?" I mused, watching Serena sway on the barstool.

He poured another shot and slid the glass to Serena. "Yep. Again, not illegal."

"I discovered Selma Greenleaf's body today out at Luna Lagoon," I said.

Donald grunted. "You don't say? Did you find the plant with her?"

"Isss tha' a queshun?" Serena slurred.

"No," I said.

"Give me that." Needles reached out and wrapped his front paws around Serena's shot glass, pulling it to him.

"No," I said. "The Lunar Blossom wasn't with her."

"Damn shame." He arched an eyebrow when I just continued to stare at him. "What? You want me to say something more?"

"Do you know where Luna Lagoon is?" I asked.

"Can't say that I do."

"Where were you last night from 9:00 to 6:00 this morning?" I asked.

Serena hiccuped and reached for the shot glass that wasn't there, her hand sliding across the bar. "Whoa! Magic! It's gone!"

"She's sloshed, Princess."

"Well?" I mused. "Where were you?"

Donald held up one hand and gestured around the room. "I was here. Opened the bar at two in the afternoon and closed it at midnight to go for a run."

I glanced around the empty bar. "How many customers did you have in here on a full-moon night? Can't be many."

He narrowed his eyes. "Just because I don't have customers don't mean I ain't open."

"So you stayed open all night until midnight?" I mused

"That's what I said."

"Did you run with someone?"

"I run alone."

I sighed. "Is there anyone who can vouch for you from midnight to 6:00 in the morning?"

"Not a soul." He smirked and shrugged. "Guess you'll just have to take my word on it, Game Warden."

🕯 12 🕯

"Just in time," Alex said as he kissed my cheek and handed me a glass of red wine. "Dinner will be ready in a few minutes."

I moaned. "Yes, to all of this." I took a gulp of the wine, and then reached up and drew his head down for a proper kiss. "You're a lifesaver."

"Tell him where we just came from and what you just did." Needles zipped into the kitchen, his wings glowing purple and green. *"Grant is gonna get you back, Princess."*

"What's Needles talking about?" Alex mused, leading me over to the kitchen island to sit on a barstool.

"We made a pit stop to interview Donald Frasier at his bar, and the blasted wolf refused to answer questions unless Serena did a shot of tequila for every question."

Alex threw back his head and laughed. "How drunk is she?"

"Let's just say it took me, Grant, *and* Mom just to get her in the house. When I left, the twins were entertaining her with a magic show." I shook my head and took another drink of wine. "Alex, there were fireworks and everything! And instead of being concerned that her *babies* could conjure up explosives at only seven months old, Serena was laughing and clapping and chasing the fireworks around the room. Much to the delight of the twins!"

"And Grant?" Alex asked, still grinning.

"He was just sitting on the couch, shaking his head. Poor guy. Less than five years ago, he was a single man living more 'normal' than 'werewolf.' Now, he's married to a witch, has twin werewitches with amazing magical abilities...and despite his look of bewilderment, he couldn't be happier."

Alex chuckled and slid a plate of veggie quiche and roasted potatoes at me. "You're probably right. I know my life has changed for the better since meeting you and your family." He slid a look at Needles. "Well, mostly for the better."

Needles lifted his paw in the air...his equivalent of shooting Alex the bird.

I laughed and picked up my plate and glass of wine and headed for the table. "Play nice, you two."

"I know the wine is a little heavy with the quiche," Alex said, "but I thought it might be needed after the day you had."

"We could be eating cereal right now, and I'd still be gulping down the red wine."

As we ate, I filled Alex in on my day. I told him about the interviews with Ella Greenleaf, Regina Hawthorn, Hannah Trueheart, Donald Frasier, and Marvina Darkstone and her PA.

"What're you thinking?" Alex mused as he pushed his empty plate aside.

"We need to find Selma's cell phone, and I find it hard to believe Ella Greenleaf wasn't concerned she never saw her grandmother. They live in the same house. Which reminds me, I think Selma's moped is still out at the lagoon somewhere. We should try to find it."

"Is that your way of saying you want to do a stakeout tonight?"

"Yep."

"We should probably visit Black Forest King tonight, Princess."

I sighed and finished off my glass of wine. "Needles is right. I know I'll see Dad tomorrow night at the party, but I should let him know what's going on. Give me an hour?"

Alex stood, gathered our plates, and nodded. "Of course. I'll fly out and get you in an hour."

I ran upstairs to change out of my uniform, and less than ten minutes later, I was jogging down the path that would lead me to Black Forest, Needles on my shoulder. As I passed Mom's cottage, I could see her silhouette through the kitchen window and knew she was probably boiling water for her nightly hot tea…and that single act brought me great comfort.

When I'd moved back to the island some three years ago, it had broken my heart to see how rundown the castle had gotten. But Mom had moved into town when I left at eighteen to join the paranormal police academy. She said it was simply too painful to live so close to my father.

And that had broken my heart. Because no two people were more in love and more destined to be together than my mother and father.

And yet…it was impossible.

"Here they come," Needles muttered, breaking me out of my melancholy thoughts.

I smiled as a ball of light came hurling my way. When it was almost upon me, it split apart and dozens of giggling fireflies clamored for my attention. That simple act also brought me great comfort.

"Princess! We're excited about the party!"

"Black Forest King is letting us attend!"

"I'm bringing berries!"

"I can't wait to see the twins!"

"Did you bring us anything?"

On and on they chattered as I jogged to the entrance of Black Forest. When I finally reached the stately pine tree that stood guard, I slowed to a stop in front of him.

"Hello, Mr. Pine. Are you excited about spring tomorrow?"

"Hello, Princess. So lovely to see you. Yes, every seasonal change is a blessing." He lifted his weighty branch. *"Enter, and have a wonderful visit with Black Forest King."*

Needles and the fireflies flew through the branches as I ducked down and entered Black Forest.

The initial impact of Black Forest is almost indescribable. It's pure euphoria—peaceful and serene. The calming effect it had on the chaos inside me always amazed me. It was the same healing presence Dad used to treat my physical and emotional wounds.

My dad was a Genius Loci. That meant he was *literally* the heart and soul of Black Forest. The protector of all the trees and animals within. As the largest tree in Black Forest, he'd stood guard over Enchanted Island for thousands of years.

Like I do every time I visit Dad, I chased after Needles and the fireflies. They would lead me to where my father stood guard. As I jumped over logs and bushes, I waved hello and called out greetings to the woodland creatures and trees.

Soon, I pushed through the clearing and saw him.

My dad.

A Genius Loci.

And the largest tree in all of Black Forest.

"Shayla! Daughter of my Heart," Dad said, his deep timbre reverberating in my head. *"I am pleased you came to see me tonight. It is growing late."*

"It's never too late to spend time with you, Dad." I levitated myself up to the base of his giant trunk and wrapped my arms around him as best I could. Resting my cheek against his rough bark, I closed my eyes and breathed him in. "I missed you."

"And I missed you as well, Daughter." I felt branches on my back, the leaves tickling me through my light-weight shirt. *"Come, tell me about your day. Your mother visited me early this morning. She said she was spending the day with GiGi and Starla."*

I stepped back and dropped down to the ground, leaning back against him. "Yep. They were working on the menu for tomorrow night's party. They gave me a taste for lunch today. All delicious."

Dad chuckled. *"I imagine it was. It will be nice to have the forest alive again with family, friends, and laughter."*

I groaned. "All I can think about are the dangerous twosomes. Do you know when I left Serena's house tonight, they were lighting *fireworks* in the house! I mean, granted, they were magical fireworks, so there wasn't any real danger of burning the house down...but still! They just started getting teeth for pity's sake!" I laughed. "They're gonna be a handful. You know that, right?" I sobered. "It scares me to think one day you may need to heal them the same way you've healed me on numerous occasions."

One of Dad's branches reached down and gently stroked my cheek. *"It always terrifies me when I am called upon to heal you, Daughter. That fear never goes away for a parent, no matter how old their child gets."*

I sighed. "Maybe I'm just feeling melancholy because of what happened today."

"And what happened?"

I told him about finding Selma Greenleaf's body out at Luna Lagoon and who our suspects were, glossing over the majority. "I guess the only good thing about this is knowing Selma never went to the north side of the island and discovered where the Lunar Blossom *really* is. I was afraid she had."

"That is *a good thing,"* Dad agreed.

"Oh, guess what? We did get some good news today. You remember Dash and Devona, right? Dash and Grant are friends and often run together when they shift, and Devona is the witch with no magical abilities, and yet she practices faithfully with Hagatha Broomly…you remember them, right?"

"I do."

"Well, they were out at Luna Lagoon last night under the full moon, and Dash proposed! And guess what? They're getting married like *fast.*" I laughed. "Mainly because they want to start a family immediately. They're having a small equinox celebration at Devona's house tomorrow night and inviting Hagatha over to tell her. They're also going to ask Hagatha to marry them."

"That is wonderful news, Daughter. It warms my heart to know they have found each other and can overcome whatever obstacles arise for them."

"It won't be easy," I said. "Even though Devona was excited, I could tell she was scared and apprehensive about whether or not their children will be werewitches or be like her and possess no magical abilities."

"We will simply hope they are blessed with healthy offspring."

I grinned. "We said the same of Serena's twins...and now look at them!"

Dad chuckled. *"Shayla, you make me laugh."*

Needles let out a whoop as he descended from Dad's branches and landed on my shoulder. *"Did you tell Black Forest King what you did to Serena tonight?"*

"Hush!" I said. "And I didn't do anything!"

"What is this?" Dad mused.

I quickly filled him in on our adventure at the bar, how it took me, Grant, and Mom to get her inside the house, and then regaled him *again* with the story of the fireworks. By the time I finished, Dad's laughter was reverberating in my head and the ground under me shook.

"This forest will be on fire within the year," Needles grumbled. *"Those little werewitches will see to it."*

"Alex Stone is flying in," Dad said. *"I guess our time together has come to an end."*

I stood and gave Dad a quick hug. "We're going on a stakeout tonight. I'm not exactly sure who we're going to spy on just yet, but it wouldn't be an investigation without a stakeout."

"Stay safe, Daughter of my Heart. I will see you tomorrow night for the spring party."

"*How long are we going to stand out here?*" Needles grumbled from my shoulder. "*We should at least peek through the windows and see if she's inside.*"

After much deliberation while flying into town, we decided to stakeout Ella Greenleaf. My position was of the six suspects, she had the most to gain with the death of Selma Greenleaf. Afterward, we'd go look for the moped out at Luna Lagoon.

"Needles is right," Alex said. "The house is dark. I'm thinking she's not here."

"*I'll go down the chimney, look around, and be right back.*"

Before we could caution him to be careful, he zipped away, his wings glowing midnight blue and silver.

"Is that really inconspicuous?" I murmured.

Alex chuckled. "Probably not."

It didn't take long before Needles returned. "*It's a mess in there! Looks like a tornado came through. She's not in any of the rooms. You gotta come see this for yourselves.*"

Looking both ways before crossing the street, Alex and I

jogged over to the Greenleaf house. Pressing my forehead against the front window, I peered inside. There was a small light on in the back of the house, which I assumed was the kitchen area. But that back light gave off enough for me to see. Needles was right. It looked like a tornado had ripped through the house. Cushions were overturned, books were upended and lying scattered on the floor, and even the furniture had been tossed around. Whoever tore through the house did not care to be gentle.

"The kitchen is even worse," Needle said as he dropped to my shoulder. *"There are broken dishes everywhere. It's like the person was in a rage."*

"So either Ella did this herself," Alex said, "or someone broke in thinking Selma had stashed the Lunar Blossom at her home and they were determined to find it."

"Does this mean someone took Ella?" I mused.

"Do you think you can do a locator spell for her?" Alex asked.

"I can try. Could be if someone *did* take her and that person can do magic, then they put a cloaking spell on her. But we'll never know unless I try."

Closing my eyes, I pictured Ella and whispered the locator spell GiGi and Mom had taught me when I was just a young witch.

My eyes popped open. "She's out at Luna Lagoon."

Alex shifted into his gargoyle form and gently scooped me in his arms, careful of his sharp talons. "Looks like we're going to Luna Lagoon."

* * *

"**D**o you suppose we'll find Ella?" I asked as Alex started to descend. "It's a large lagoon."

We were almost on the ground when a bright light lit up the surrounding area…followed by shouts and screams.

"What the heck?" I jumped out of Alex's arms, his feet barely on the ground before I took off running. "I can sense magic."

Alex shifted back to his human form and easily caught up with me. Needles' wings were fluttering so fast on my shoulder, one wing kept tickling my neck. A sure sign he was itching for a fight.

"What are you doing out here?" a female voice screeched. "My grandma wouldn't want you out here snatching up her Lunar Blossom."

Another burst of light and another round of screams and curses lit up the night sky as I slowed to a stop.

"It's Ella," I said, feeling ridiculous for stating the obvious.

An amused laugh rang out. "Your magic is no match for me, you silly little witch. Don't even try it. I'll wipe the floor with you."

"And that's Regina Hawthorn," I said.

"A witch fight! All right! My money's on Regina. That Ella is scrappy, but Regina's right, her magic is better."

"We aren't betting on a witch fight," I said exasperatingly.

Alex chuckled. "Guess we'll be breaking up a fight on our stakeout tonight."

"Lovely," I muttered.

Alex winked at me, then cupped his hands over his mouth. "This is the Enchanted Island Sheriff's Department. Do *not* engage in magic, or we will shoot!"

I scoffed. "We don't have any weapons on us."

"They don't know that."

We jogged across the grass and rocks, moving aside over-sized leaves that got in our way until we came to where the two women stood…breathing heavily and facing off with each other.

"No one should be out here," Alex said. "This is a crime scene."

"He's right," I said. "What are you two doing out here?"

"I'm looking for my grandma's moped," Ella said. "That's it."

"Down here by the shore? Really?" I turned to Regina Hawthorn. "And you?"

"I'm looking for the *real* Lunar Blossom, and if I happen to stumble over the hybrid Selma was trying to pawn off, I might snag some of that as well. I'm itching to see what she cross polli-nated and how it works."

Ella lifted her fists in the air. "If my grandma said she found the Lunar Blossom, then she found the Lunar Blossom."

"No," I said to Regina, ignoring Ella's outburst. "Until we know exactly what flowers were used, I'm going to caution you away from the hybrid."

Regina scowled. "You're just trying to keep it for yourself."

Needles leaped off my shoulder, whipped out a quill from his back, and zipped over to Regina, his wings glowing bright red. *"You will want to back down, Witch!"*

"Nobody is doing any searching tonight," Alex growled. "You." He pointed to Regina. "Go home."

I could tell Regina wanted to argue…but common sense won out. Huffing, she whipped around and stomped off in the oppo-site direction.

"Good riddance," Ella muttered.

Alex crossed his arms and glared at Ella. "You are not to take anything from this location. That includes your grandmother's moped. Seems to me, if you were that worried about it, you'd look for it in the daylight. Not at night. Now, go home. Shayla and I stopped by to check on you tonight, and we noticed the state of your home. What happened?"

"Nothing. I misplaced something is all." Without saying another word, Ella strode past us, muttering to herself the entire time.

"Yeah! Keep walking, Witch!" Needles shouted to Ella's back, brandishing his quill in the air.

"Well," I said, "this was a colossal waste of time."

"Maybe not," Alex said. "I find it interesting both women were out here searching for whatever it was Selma had."

"You think one of them is the killer? Maybe came out here to see if they could find more of the hybrid they already stole from Selma?"

"Seems plausible."

"I'm exhausted, Princess." Needles landed on my shoulder, his wings glowing gray and blue. *"We're never going to find the moped in the dark. Let's go home."*

❧ 14 ☙

Needles and I rode into town with Alex the next morning. The autopsy and forensic reports were ready to go, so we skipped the bakery and drove straight for the sheriff's station. Parking along the street, I opened the front door and stepped inside. To the left was a set of stairs leading upstairs to the sheriff's office, and to the right was a set of stairs leading down to the laboratories. Needles gave me a salute and headed upstairs for the sheriff's station.

He never attended an autopsy meeting.

"Think Pearl is here?" I whispered as Alex and I descended the stairs.

I had this sort of fake snarky thing going with Pearl. She wasn't near as mean as she liked us to believe...and I enjoyed giving her a hard time.

Sure enough, sitting behind an old wooden desk was Mrs. Pearl Earthly-Caraway—the octogenarian witch who guarded the labs like a dragon guards his treasure. When she saw us, she scowled and shook her finger.

"I was about to put out an APB on you two," she snapped. "Doc, Finn, and Grant are waiting for you both." She made a point to look at the clock on the wall. "It's ten after eight. You're late."

"Well," I said, "it's a good thing we don't—"

"Thank you, Mrs. Earthly-Caraway," Alex interrupted. "I was unaware of the time. If you'd please let Doc know we are here, I'd appreciate it."

"Or we can just walk back," I muttered.

"Humph!" Pearl said. "No one goes back until I clear them." She narrowed her eyes and looked first at me, then Alex, then back at me. "No matter who they are."

"How's that retirement plan coming along?" I asked chipperly. "Have you given anymore thought to it?"

Alex let out a bark of laughter...then tried to smother it with a cough.

"You think you're funny, Shayla Loci-Stone?" Pearl asked. "Well, you won't be laughing when you wake up with a sudden case of laryngitis and acne."

Because I knew the powerful old witch could do it...I simply gave her a tight smile.

"How's that call coming?" Alex mused.

"Don't rush me!" Pearl snapped. "You young people are always in a hurry."

It was all I could do not to point out she'd just chewed our butts out for being ten minutes late.

When she hung up and motioned for us to go on back, I gave her a two-finger wave. "Tootles."

"Tootles," Pearl muttered. "What kind of greeting is that for a game warden to give?"

"A happy-first-day-of-spring greeting," I said.

Pearl's lips twitched in amusement, but she refused to out-right smile.

"Why do you insist on goading her?" Alex asked when we were halfway down the hallway.

"Because she likes it. I've met her husband. He's about the sweetest little kitchen witch I ever met outside of Serena and Tamara. No way he stands up to her. She needs someone to snipe at. Trust me on that."

Shaking his head, Alex knocked once on Doc's door before pushing it open.

Sure enough, Doc, Finn, and Grant were already in the lab. We took a few minutes to exchange pleasantries, and I couldn't help but ask Grant how Serena was feeling.

He grinned. "She was a little hungover this morning, but not too bad. She still made it to the bakery by five."

"I need to hear this story," Finn said.

I laughed. "I'll let Serena tell you tonight. You're still coming, right?"

"Jordan and I will be there," Finn said.

"I'll be there as well," Doc said. "It's time I started accepting more invitations out."

I knew what he was saying. A while back, the woman Doc had been seeing was murdered, and when it was revealed the only reason she was targeted was because the killer hated Doc... well, Doc still hadn't fully recovered from that blow.

"I'm sure you all have a busy day," Doc said. "Let's go ahead and get started." He led us over to the body. "Selma Greenleaf, eighty-two-year-old witch, died from a blow to the head—blunt force trauma. You can see here the pattern from the object." He pointed to the left side of her skull. "The Riverstone rock found at the scene was a perfect match. Blood on the rock came back as Selma's as well. I put time of death between midnight and one."

"Two things," Finn said. "One, the rock was too porous for me to get fingerprints from. Sorry about that. The other thing is slightly frightening. I looked at the properties of the flowers found in Selma's fist, and I have found traces of Moonflower and Night-Blooming Jasmine. In and of themselves, great healing flowers." She caught my eyes, and I knew whatever she was going to say next would be critical to our case. "But, Shayla, I also found trace amounts of Devil's Snare."

I sucked in a ragged breath. "Why would she add that? That's beyond dangerous."

"What's Devil's Snare?" Grant asked.

"Devil's Snare is only one name," Finn said. "It also goes by Devil's Trumpet, jimsonweed, and thorn apple. Basically, if ingested in large doses, it can cause hallucinations, paranoia, confusion, explosive behavior, dry mouth, and tachycardia to name just a few side effects."

Alex snorted. "We saw a lot of those symptoms from two of our suspects last night during our stakeout."

I nodded. "We did. Plus, Needles and I saw that behavior in Marvina Darkstone too. In the blink of an eye, she destroyed her living room. And according to Marvina's PA, Hazel Birchwood, Selma gave Marvina liquid samples of her hybrid. If all three of them have ingested Selma's hybrid flower, then it's only a matter of time before they go off the rails." I glared down at the dead body of Selma Greenleaf. "What the heck were you thinking, Selma?"

"She had to have known, right?" Grant asked.

I snorted. "Yes. Even a novice witch knows harmful plants and flowers."

"Why would she sell it to her granddaughter?" Alex mused. "Much less anyone else? That makes no sense."

"I may have that answer," Doc said. "I found recent deterioration of certain vital organs. It was slight, but it had me stumped for a bit until Selma's tox report came back. She was sampling her hybrid. Not long, mind you. Less than a month, I'd say."

"We should check with Ella," I said. "See if she noticed a change in her grandma's behavior." I shrugged. "Although, having spoken with Ella on a couple different occasions, I'm not sure she'd have noticed anything outside of her little bubble."

Doc smiled. "Self-absorbed?"

"Yes," I said. "She can't seem to get past the fact Selma was making her bid on the flower and not just giving it to her outright."

"Which, thank the goddess, she didn't," Finn said. "Can you imagine what would have happened if Ella had used this hybrid in her tea blends at the shop?"

I glanced at Alex. "Who's saying she isn't? If she *is* our killer, and we suspect the killer got away with the stash Selma was hoarding..." I shook my head and sighed. "We need to get a handle on this and find our killer fast before other citizens get hurt."

"I have backgrounds ready," Grant said.

"Good luck today," Doc said.

I smiled. "Thanks. And we'll see you both tonight out at Black Forest for the celebration."

15

Opal Earthly-Caraway looked up from her computer when Alex, Grant, and I strolled through the doors of the sheriff's office. "Good morning, Sheriff. Detective Wolfe. And, Shayla, so lovely to see you."

Opal was completely different from her twin sister, Pearl… and it showed. "Thank you, Opal. I love that brooch. Very spring-like."

Tears filled Opal's eyes. "Thank you. It was a gift from my husband. Hard to believe it'll be two years this October for all four of us."

Opal and Pearl had married twin brothers after the Samhain festival a year and a half ago…the first marriage for all four of them! The Enchanted Island citizens had come out in droves for that long-awaited party.

"We're down to one bag of pretzels," Needles said as he flew in from the lounge, his wings glowing black and gray. *"I can't be expected to solve this case if I'm not properly fed!"*

"I'll see what I can do," I said dryly.

"I stopped by the bakery on my way in," Grant said. "Serena tossed in a caramel pretzel for you, Needles."

"Bless that tequila-chugging witch. At least someone cares about me."

The three of us made our way to Grant's desk, and while he opened the box from Enchanted Bakery & Brew, Alex slid two chairs in front of Grant's desk while I ran and got us all coffee.

"Looks like there are cinnamon rolls, cranberry-orange muffins, and a caramel-dipped pretzel rod." Grant tossed Needles a pretzel, then handed Alex a cinnamon roll before taking a huge bite of his own roll. "Man, my wife sure can bake."

"I bet you wished you could say the same thing, Gargoyle." Needles laughed and did a flip in the air, his wings glowing purple and green.

"Keep it up," I warned, setting the three coffees down on Grant's desk, "and I'll forget to pick up more bags of pretzels at the store." I reached into the box and took out a cranberry-orange muffin.

"Okay," Grant said, licking his fingers clean, and then wiping them off with a napkin. "Here's what I got from PADA and from pulling some Enchanted Island records. Selma Greenleaf, witch. Eighty-two years old. Widowed, one child deceased. Moved to Enchanted Island some fifty years ago with her then-alive husband. She worked as an herbalist and healer most of her life. She owned her home outright, and her financials were fairly solid. She took out a loan to help her granddaughter open her tea shop. No criminal record on file."

"According to our reports," I said, "Selma was going around the island telling people she'd found one of the most elusive plants in existence—the Lunar Blossom. I know for a fact there's only one of those plants on the island, and it's on the north side. So, of course, I was upset when I heard this. Anyway, Selma was trying to get a bidding war going. Upon further investigation, we've discovered Selma lied. What she did was make a hybrid flower. She used three different flowers. Two of those flowers aren't bad in and of themselves…except one of the flowers, the Devil's Snare, is like taking a highly addictive drug."

"She used Devil's Snare?" Needles demanded. *"No wonder we got supernaturals acting all emotional and angry."*

"It does blow my mind," Alex agreed. "A woman who was supposed to be a healer was willing to give someone toxic flowers."

I nodded. "Yeah. I'm still reeling from that as well. Anyway, Selma did her homework. Trying to pawn off the hybrid as the Lunar Blossom, Selma contacted two supernaturals whose businesses were struggling financially and who could reap the benefits of the elusive Lunar Blossom."

"And what are those benefits?" Grant asked.

"The true Lunar Blossom can help the skin look younger and fresher. So for non-magicals who can't just throw up a glamour, this would be beneficial. Hence, why she contacted a spa owner named Hannah Trueheart. Another odd benefit is if properly extracted, the oil extract from the flower can be added to booze and it somehow makes the booze three times more potent."

"Which would benefit bar owners," Alex said.

"Yep," I agreed. "That's why she sought out Donald Frasier."

"And the other suspects?" Grant asked.

"One was her own granddaughter, Ella Greenleaf, who just opened her own tea shop, and another is an herbalist, Regina Hawthorn, who was kicked out of her coven for shady practices. And, I'll be honest, I still don't understand why Selma contacted her. Regina would know the plant wasn't authentic." I lifted a hand in the air. "Who knows? Anyway, the last person Selma contacted was an artist by the name of Marvina Darkstone. I've put both her *and* her personal assistant on our list now. So those are the six suspects."

Grant glanced down at the paper in his hand. "First up is Ella Greenleaf, witch. Age, twenty-four. Single, no kids. Born on Enchanted Island. Mother died when Ella was five. Grandmother, Selma Greenleaf, took her in. Ella owns Teas, Tinctures, & Tonics, a fairly new store on Enchanted Island. Major debt to her name, both for the business and in her personal life. She was expelled from a supernatural college a couple years ago when she hexed a rival witch who was up for the same head sorority position. The other girl's parents pressed charges with the local paranormal police department and Ella was given a citation for misuse of magic and endangering other supernaturals. Along with being kicked out of college, she received community service and was put on probation for three years."

"What was the hex?" I asked. "Does it say?"

Grant nodded, his lips twitching. "Oh, yeah. She made the other girl's hair fall out, and then she caused her to have temporary amnesia during her presentation. Unfortunately, the hex got out of control, and it also ran to the other sorority sisters. They all lost their hair and had temporary memory loss as well."

"Now that's what I call a hex!"

I couldn't help the bark of laughter that escaped. "You've got to be kidding? Yeah, I can see where that caused her some problems." I took a sip of my coffee. "Tommy told me Ella's grand opening didn't go smoothly. It seems she made an elixir for a female werewolf to get rid of unwanted hair, and *all* the woman's body hair fell out."

"Motive for Ella?" Alex asked.

"Tommy said Ella came into his bar the night of the full moon, angry and telling him she thought it unfair her grandmother was making her bid on the Lunar Blossom. She felt it should have been given to her. Obviously, she was angry enough Tommy felt it important to let me know—well, that *and* he wanted me to know Selma was trying to sell the elusive Lunar Blossom. Anyway, when Needles and I went to see Ella *before* I discovered her grandmother's body, I'd say Tommy was spot on. She was still angry about the flower. So much so, she was convinced her grandmother had double-crossed her by eliminating her from even bidding on the flower because she hadn't heard from her grandmother all day. Of course, now we know it was because Selma was dead. But I have no problem imagining Ella angry enough to kill her own grandmother."

Grant took a sip of his coffee. "And when you told Ella her grandmother was dead?"

Needles snorted. *"Cold. She didn't even blink an eye. She just wanted to know about the plant, and if it was found, would she be given rights to it because she was next of kin."*

"So she's a contender for lead suspect?" Alex deadpanned.

I grinned. "Yeah, she's a contender."

"Alibi?" Alex mused.

"She was at Boos & Brews until 11:00 on the night of the murder. She then claims to have driven out to the northwest side of the island to gather moon ingredients for her teas until 1:00 in the morning. Unfortunately, no one can corroborate this. She returned home, went straight to bed, then got up the next morning—didn't see her grandma, but wasn't concerned—and left for work."

Alex snatched another cinnamon roll from the box. "Motive?"

"Livid her grandma was going to make her bid on the

supposed Lunar Blossom. She came across as very entitled when I spoke to her. She told me she should have been given the plant —or at least one of its flowers—for free since she was the grand-daughter. Again, when I told her Selma was dead, her first question was about the plant."

"Next up," Grant said, "I have Donald Frasier, werewolf. Age, fifty-seven. Moved to Enchanted Island five years ago. He owns Howling at the Moon, a bar on the east side of the island. He does have a criminal record. Nine years ago, he was arrested when his previous bar—also called Howling at the Moon—was raided by local supernatural police. They confiscated a large amount of Lupine Elixir."

"What exactly is that?" Alex asked. "A stimulant or drug of some kind?"

Grant nodded. "Yeah. It's a temporary concoction that amplifies a werewolf's physical strength and agility. Very addictive, and high doses can result in a frenzied state wherein the werewolf loses control and can do serious bodily harm. Donald was sentenced to two years in jail. He had to sell his bar, of course. Once he got out, he did his year probation, and then moved here. He's been open for about six months now, and from what I can tell from his financials, he's in danger of losing the bar already. Heavily in debt and running in the red."

"I don't like bad guys coming to my island," Needles said. *"Even if he did give Serena free drinks last night."*

I smiled. "Again, Grant, I'm so sorry."

He laughed. "She needs to blow off steam sometimes. It's all good."

"Motive?" Alex asked.

"Tommy Trollman told me Donald's bar isn't doing well," I said. "Tommy didn't come out and say it, but if I had to guess,

I'd say Donald Frasier may have asked Tommy for a personal loan."

"And Tommy said no?" Alex mused. "That's not very sound business on his part. Especially if this Donald guy forfeits on the loan. Tommy could gain another bar."

"Tommy doesn't deal with known criminals," I said emphatically. "No matter what it might gain him."

"If Donald's bar is in dire straits," Grant said, "I can see why he'd want to get his hands on the Lunar Blossom—or supposed Lunar Blossom—no matter the cost."

I nodded. "Exactly. Just one drop of pure extract from the flower can make a bottle of alcohol have three times its potency. He can pour watered-down drinks and keep the same bottle going for way longer. It would greatly help his non-existent profit margin."

"And alibi?" Alex asked.

"He told Serena, Needles, and me he was at the bar until closing, which was around midnight since it was a full moon."

"But?" Alex mused.

"Needles can back me up here," I said. "That place was dead last night when we went in. There was one guy in there—and he was passed out. I can't image it was any different the night of a full moon. Why stay open if you have no customers? Also, it was the way he answered the questions. And I'm not talking about making Serena drink. I'm talking about his tone. It was almost like he dared me to call him on the lie. I don't think he was being completely truthful. But, again, I can't prove it."

"Could be he closed the bar early and went for a run under the full moon," Grant said. "But with that not being a very good alibi, *and* he has a criminal record, it could be he decided to lie and claim he was at work."

I nodded. "I can see that."

Needles whipped out a quill from his back. *"He'd tell the truth if I had a go at him. Twenty seconds...that's all I'd need."*

Grant smiled as he shifted papers. "Next, I have Marvina Darkstone, vampire. Seventy-two years old. Widowed twice, no children. Has lived on Enchanted Island for six years now. Well-known supernatural artist. Excellent financials. No criminal history."

"Motive?" Alex asked.

I took a sip of my coffee. "Marvina is addicted to her 'enhancements' as her PA called them. She lives in a constantly altered state, from what I saw. Selma Greenleaf approached Marvina and said she had access to the Lunar Blossom, promising Marvina it would help her focus and create faster paintings. She then gave Marvina a little sample. We now know what she probably gave Marvina was the hybrid, which would explain Marvina's erratic behavior over the last week, according to her PA."

"Is she famous?" Grant mused. "I'm not into art, so I've never heard of her."

I nodded. "Yes. I recognized Marvina's work as soon as I saw paintings on her walls. Supernatural museums stateside and overseas showcase her work."

"Unfortunately," Alex said, "it wouldn't be the first time I've heard of a creative who needs a little juicing to get in the mood."

Grant nodded. "True. You just don't really think of it happening on Enchanted Island."

I finished off the last of my muffin and brushed the crumbs off my fingertips. "Like I said, Marvina's a hot mess. She could barely function—paranoid, angry, depressive. At first, when I asked Marvina about Selma and the Lunar Blossom, she was enraged Selma hadn't contacted her yet. Then, when I told her Selma was dead and there was no Lunar Blossom, she totally lost it. She zipped around the room before I could even blink and started throwing things against the wall, screaming and crying. Her PA ran in, demanding to know what was going on."

"It was the most tragically entertaining thing I'd seen in a while," Needles said around a mouthful of pretzel.

"So is there motive to kill her supplier?" Alex mused.

I shrugged. "I don't know. Marvina's a tough one to figure out. Maybe she thought by killing Selma she could keep the plant for herself and not spend any money to obtain it. Yet, she assured me she was willing to pay any price."

"Did she have the presence of mind to kill Selma?" Grant mused. "Your description of her left me confused."

I laughed. "That's pretty much Marvina in a nutshell. If hopped up on enhancements, I'd say yes. If Marvina was 'sober,' then I'd say no way. She didn't even have the drive to get up off the couch when she was sober. Oh, one other thing. I noticed a bandage on Marvina's hand. I asked her what happened, but she couldn't remember. Claimed she probably cut it on one of her tools while painting."

"Alibi?" Alex asked.

"Hazel, the PA, gave me the alibi for both of them. Mainly because by this time in the interview, Marvina was back to being hopped up on the Museleaf drink Hazel had given her."

"What's that?" Alex asked.

I peered into the bakery box to steal another muffin, but thought better of it. "Museleaf leaves the imbiber in a dream-like state, leaving them free to let their creativity go. So by then, Marvina was humming to herself and not able to answer my questions. Hazel told me both she and Marvina were home the night of the full moon. I guess Marvina had taken the last of the sample Selma had left, so Marvina was in an altered state and worked until two that morning. Hazel said she was there watching over Marvina."

"Does she live there?" Grant asked.

"Hazel? Yes." I snorted. "As you can imagine, someone like Marvina would need constant supervision."

"Speaking of Hazel Birchwood," Grant said, glancing down at his notes. "She's a twenty-seven-year-old witch. Single, no children. Moved back to Enchanted Island after college. She has a degree in art history. Her financials aren't that great, but no major debt outside of school loans. No criminal history."

I sighed. "I will admit I got a little short with Hazel at one point in the interview. She tells me her father's side of the family isn't from Enchanted Island, but her mother and grandmother are both here *and* they're healers and make potions for others. I just lost it. I asked her how she could knowingly allow Marvina to consume Selma's samples knowing what she does about the island."

"What did she say?" Alex asked.

"That she was told when she first got the job as PA that if she *didn't* supply Marvina with enhancements, then she could find another job." I shrugged. "And I guess I understand. Hazel swore to me she only gives Marvina natural enhancements, but when Selma came by and gave Marvina the hybrid samples, there was nothing Hazel could do. And, in Hazel's defense, she didn't know it wasn't the Lunar Blossom Selma said she had."

"I still say Hazel's an enabler," Needles said. *"And she definitely needs to be a suspect."*

"Motive for Hazel to kill Selma is a little trickier," I said. "Maybe deep down she was pissed Selma had given Marvina the sample, but then again, in her own words, Hazel said Marvina was able to finish three pieces in record time. So I don't know why Hazel would kill Selma."

"Unless it's the same as Marvina," Grant said. "Could be Hazel wanted to eliminate the middleman. Take out Selma and keep the plant for herself. If Hazel's mother and grandmother are healers, perhaps they could help her cultivate what she had and keep Marvina supplied."

"I like it," I said. "Same alibi for both women. They were home the entire night, and Hazel babysat Marvina until two o'clock in the morning."

"Next is Regina Hawthorn, witch. Age, fifty-six. Divorced, no children. Born and raised on Enchanted Island. Owner of Regina's Remedies, which she runs out of her house. Six years ago, Sheriff Hawkins arrested her for distribution of a potion without proper warning. She was selling Dreamer's Thistle. According to my notes, it's used for insomnia, but Regina didn't tell her customers the ingredients, and many were found in a paralyzed state, and a few even slipped into a one-day coma. No one was fatally injured, but it was serious enough she was arrested for unauthorized distribution of a controlled substance and negligence and spent a month in jail."

I nodded. "GiGi said she was kicked out of her coven after she went to jail."

"That's not all." Grant smiled at me. "I see you know Regina personally."

"I gave her a misdemeanor citation about a year ago for unauthorized harvesting of magical herbs. Caught her on the edge of the north border around the river."

"I still say we should have cut off a few of her fingers back then. That would have made an impression."

"The PADA paperwork on that would have been a logistical nightmare," Alex deadpanned. "Okay, so Regina's motive?"

I grinned and shook my head at Alex's joke. "Selma approached Regina and said she had the Lunar Blossom and said she was taking bids for it. Ella Greenleaf told me she saw Regina and Selma fighting in her front yard the night Selma was murdered. When I asked Regina about it, she admitted she went out to Selma's house to demand proof of the flower. When Selma showed her a picture, Regina said she knew immediately it wasn't the Lunar Blossom. She admitted she wasn't exactly sure *what* it was, but it wasn't the Lunar Blossom. She called Selma out on her lie and left. That confrontation happened around 7:00 or 7:30, according to both Regina and Ella."

"And Regina's alibi?" Alex mused.

"Regina claims she was down on the south end foraging for moon mushrooms and night-bloom flowers for a potion she's making. She got home before midnight. Again, no one can corroborate this because she lives alone."

Grant finished the last of his coffee. "Our final suspect is Hannah Trueheart, fairy. Age, forty-four. Married, two adult children. Moved to Enchanted Island with her husband and two kids eleven years ago. Owns Tranquil Tides on the south side of the island. It's only been open for about a year now. Lots of business debt. Personal debt is under control. No criminal record."

"Her motive?" Alex asked.

"This is a difficult one as well," I said. "Hannah claims Selma went to her business last week. Said she'd done her research and knew of the four spas on the island, Hannah's was the one struggling the most. She then made the same offer she made to the other suspects. Highest bidder gets the plant and its flowers. Hannah told me she told Selma to take a hike. She wasn't interested."

"And the business card we found in Selma's pocket?" Alex asked.

"Hannah said Selma took it when she was at the spa last week—just in case. As to how it ended up in Selma's pocket the night of the murder? I don't know. Maybe that's the dress Selma wore to the spa, and she just didn't wash the dress and then wore it again on the night she was murdered? I'm not sure. I can tell you of all the suspects, Hannah seemed the most insistent she didn't want it. I'm not sure if Hannah had a motive or not to want Selma dead. Unless she's just saying that to throw me off her trail."

"And her alibi?" Alex asked.

"It's fairly solid. At least, compared to the others. She and her husband went to visit their oldest son's family that night. They'd just had a baby a few weeks back, and this was the first time Hannah had gotten away from the spa at a decent hour to go visit. They stayed until 8:00. Afterward, they went to High Seas Bar & Grill to have a celebratory drink for being grandparents. They stayed at High Seas until around 9:30, and then they went home. She said she was too exhausted to do even simple spell work under the full moon, so she and her husband just went to bed."

"I can call High Seas for you," Grant offered. "I know that's not within the time of death for Selma, but it might help."

"Thanks. I'd appreciate that." I turned to Alex. "I'd like to pay another visit to Donald Frasier now that we know his extensive criminal background."

Alex grinned. "Are you saying you'd like company today?"

"We got this, Gargoyle."

I shot Needles a look before nodding. "Yeah. I'd like company for the day."

Needles threw up his paws. *"And here I thought it was going to be a glorious first day of spring!"*

"I feel like Hannah Trueheart might be our weakest suspect," I said, ignoring Needles. "Ella Greenleaf and Regina Hawthorn were extremely worked up last night out at Luna Lagoon. If one of them is the killer and they're sampling the hybrid, we might be able to tell more today if they're experiencing consumption symptoms from the Devil's Snare. I also want to make sure Hazel throws out any samples they may still have lingering around Marvina's house."

Grant nodded. "I'll text about the Trueheart alibi when I get confirmation from High Seas Bar & Grill."

16

Since we were already in town, we decided to stop at Teas, Tinctures, & Tonics first. I thought maybe Ella wouldn't have the store open since she'd be knee-deep in funeral preparations…so I was mildly surprised when we pulled to a stop in front of the store, and the open sign was flashing.

Alex pulled the door open, and Needles and I entered ahead of him. Ella was standing by the tonics area yelling at the older witch behind the counter. I'd have taken exception with her behavior if the old witch looked upset—but she didn't. Mainly, she just looked bored.

"I gotta say," I said. "I'm a little surprised to see you open today, Ella."

Ella whirled around and glared. "Why would I be closed? I have a business to run. Granny would understand."

"I was just telling Miss Ella how happy I was to hear about Devona Flame and her young man," the elderly witch said, a twinkle in her eye. "I know it's supposed to be a secret until they get a chance to tell Hagatha tonight, but my granddaughter told me about it."

"Why should I care if a normal gets married?" Ella demanded. "It's not like she's a true witch."

"Less than a minute in, and I already want to stab her with a quill."

I agreed wholeheartedly. "You look a little tired, Ella. You feeling okay?"

"No, I'm not feeling okay. I didn't sleep well last night. My grandma has been *murdered,* in case you've forgotten." She rested an elbow on the counter and rubbed her head. "And I can't seem to get rid of this headache."

I exchanged a knowing look with Alex.

"I just offered to make her an herbal tea," the older witch rasped. "That'll help."

"Really?" Ella snapped, lifting her head. "Is herbal tea gonna help me find Granny's will, Beulah? Because I don't think it will."

Beulah arched an eyebrow. "It might help with that acerbic tongue of yours."

Needles laughed. *"You tell her!"*

"Is that what you were looking for last night?" I asked. "Your house looked like it has been tossed by a thief."

"Not that it's any of your business, but yes. I need to find her will."

Needles whipped out a quill from his back and proceeded to clean his paw with the sharp instrument...his eyes never leaving Ella.

She must've understood the silent threat because she shuffled her feet and looked away. "I spent all night searching the house from top to bottom. I've no idea where Granny's will is. I have no idea what becomes of the house, what becomes of me now that she took out a loan to help me start this business." She threw up her hands in disgust. "Could she have chosen a more inopportune time to die? I doubt it."

"That's reason 10,563 why I'll never have kids, Princess. In case you're keeping count."

"Did she have a lawyer?" Alex asked.

"How the heck would I know?" Ella demanded. "The woman was tight-lipped about everything. Including the Lunar Blossom. I bet she did that on purpose. I bet she's getting a big laugh right now, wherever she's at. Thinking she's pulled one over on me."

"Is this the crazy and paranoid part we're supposed to be looking for?"

I bit my lip so I wouldn't laugh out loud.

"You know," Ella said, pulling out her phone. "I got a call at five o'clock last night from a number I didn't recognize. I didn't answer it because it could have been anyone. Do you think it might have been Granny's lawyer? Why didn't they leave a message?" She looked up at me, her pupils huge and dilated. "Do you think it was the lawyer?"

"Only one way to find out," I said. "But before you do that, I need to ask you a quick question."

Ella huffed. "Make it fast. I'm very busy right now."

Beulah snorted.

"Over the last three weeks before your grandmother died," I said, "did you notice a change in her behavior?"

"She was more secretive and mean. Making me, her only grandchild, bid on something that should have just been given to me. Like I was some sort of stranger to her."

I rolled my eyes, tired of her same song and dance. "I'm looking for something more specific. Maybe erratic behavior like explosive anger, or maybe she was showing signs of paranoia? Was she having trouble sleeping or complaining of headaches?"

Ella frowned, and her brows drew together. "I don't know. Maybe. She was yelling a lot more, I do know that. There were a couple times when I woke up in the middle of the night and she was pacing in the kitchen, muttering to herself. She didn't normally do that, but I just figured she was getting old. Senile. Wasn't until she mentioned having the Lunar Blossom that I realized she'd been keeping a secret from me."

"One last thing," I said. "When we ran your background, we noticed you'd been expelled from college for hexing a fellow sorority sister. Unfortunately, the hex went wrong, and it affected your other sorority sisters as well. You were charged for that, weren't you?"

Ella scowled. "Obviously, since you read it in my background report."

I gave her a tight-lipped smile. "It makes me wonder just how far you'd go to get what you want. Would you go so far as to kill your own grandmother?"

Without waiting for a reply, I nodded once to Beulah before turning to leave—Needles laughing in my ear and Alex falling into step beside me. It wasn't until I reached the front door that I heard Ella cry out.

"Of course I wouldn't kill my own grandmother!"

17

Regina Hawthorn opened the front door of her house and frowned. "I didn't go back out to the lagoon last night, and I haven't contacted Ella. What now?"

"We just need to ask you a couple questions," I said.

On the way out to Regina's house, Alex and I had gone over what it was we were going to say to Regina. We didn't really need answers, we just wanted to gauge her reaction to our questions. Like with Ella, we were looking for signs she might be using the hybrid.

"Well, I suppose I should have you come in then." She motioned us inside, and as she shut the door, a tea kettle went off somewhere in the back of the house. "Oh, goddess above! I totally forgot I had the teakettle on."

Turning on her heel, she hurried out of the room. Alex and I followed behind her down a hallway and into a cheerful-looking kitchen. The mid-morning sunlight streamed through herb-filled windowsills and fell onto the rustic wooden countertops. I'd done the same thing in my kitchen when I'd remodeled a few years ago. Wooden countertops were definitely the way to go. Lavender and rosemary permeated the air as Regina motioned for us to take a seat at the kitchen table.

"Can I get you something to drink?" she asked, pulling the kettle off the stove.

"No, thanks," I said. "We just had coffee."

Needles flew up and perched on the light fixture above the table. I knew he'd be keeping a lookout for anything out of the ordinary from his high position.

"I have two large orders I need to fill today," Regina said. "I'm a little scattered." She dumped two huge tablespoons of something into a tea strainer before lowering it into her hot water. Reaching over with her left hand, she flipped an hourglass over and brought it and her hot mug of tea with her to the table. "I like to steep my tea to a precise time."

"Why do you think Selma offered you the Lunar Blossom?" I asked. "I just can't understand that. She had to have known you'd know it was a scam."

Irritation flittered over Regina's features...but I couldn't tell if it was meant for me because I was being nosy or if she was still sore at almost being taken for a fool by Selma.

"I don't know. I've thought about that myself." When the sand in the hourglass ran out, Regina picked up her mug and blew on it before taking a sip. I didn't miss the slight tremor in her hands. "Maybe she was just trying to muster up some excitement with the other prospective buyers. You know, tell them she had more people interested in the flower than she really had."

Alex nodded. "Could be. Could also be she didn't figure you'd cry foul if you *were* taken advantage of."

Regina scowled and slammed her mug on the kitchen table. "What's that supposed to mean?"

"Nice one, Gargoyle."

Alex shrugged nonchalantly. "You know, since you have a criminal record *and* you've been kicked out of your coven."

"Do you have a specific reason for being here?" Regina demanded. "Other than to harass me?"

I shook my head. "Not really. We just wanted to remind you that Luna Lagoon was still off limits. You aren't to go out there until we say."

"It's the spring equinox," Regina said between clenched teeth. "I have plenty to do today *and* tonight."

I nodded and stood, Needles drifting down to land on my shoulder. "Then we'll let you get to it."

"We can see ourselves out," Alex said.

* * *

We decided to stop by Luna Lagoon before heading to talk to Marvina and Hazel. I wanted to take another look around the crime scene and see if we couldn't find Selma's moped, now that it was light outside.

"I think I'll just stay here and nap on top of the roof," Needles said. *"It's the first day of spring. I should be sunbathing. Spike likes it when my quills are tan."*

I snorted. Needles' girlfriend, Spike, lived in the Bermuda Triangle. It was a long-distance relationship, but it seemed to be working for them. They made sure to talk over Broom Chat at least once a week.

We left Needles basking in the sun as we trudged through the deep foliage toward the lagoon. Five minutes later, we stepped into the clearing near the area where Selma's body had been discovered.

"Do you want to fan out and look for the moped?" I asked.

Alex grinned. "Or I could just shift and fly around and look for it from above."

I laughed and barely refrained from smacking my head. "Yeah, or you can do that."

A furry wet head popped up out of the lagoon near the edge. *"Hello. Remember me?"*

I stopped and put my hand on Alex's arm. "My friend Olly is here. Hey, Olly. Enjoying your swim?"

"Sure am. What're you doing here? Have you come to play?"

"We're looking for a moped," I said. "That's a small, two-wheeled vehicle. Have you seen anything like that parked around here? Maybe in the bushes?"

"I sure have!" He ducked under the water and popped up again near the edge of the lagoon. Crawling out of the water, he shook the water off before scrambling up the small embankment. *"Want me to show you?"*

"That would be great, Olly. Thanks."

Alex and I scurried to keep up with the sleek little animal. Because his back legs were a tiny bit longer than his front legs, he ran with a cute little hopping gait.

"Over this way!" he shouted as he stood up on his hind legs and clapped his front paws overhead.

"He sure can move," Alex laughed.

We followed Olly for another thirty yards, over gnarled mangrove roots and through thick foliage, until we finally came to a stop near a dense cluster of bromeliads.

"It's in there," Olly said.

It was easy to spot now that we were on top of the yellow moped. Selma must have driven in from the back side of the foliage because there were no tracks or signs otherwise.

"How did she get it back here?" Alex mused.

I laughed. "I was wondering the same thing. I can use my magic and levitate it out."

"Or I can just lift it out. It can't weigh but two hundred pounds."

"It's okay, He-Man. I can just levitate it out."

He sent me a grin and shrugged. "Not often I get to flex my muscles for you."

Shaking my head and laughing, I used my magic and levitated the yellow moped out from the thick foliage and set it down in front of us.

"Cute basket," Alex said.

Positioned in front of the moped was a white woven basket with bright plastic flowers. The kind of small baskets bicycles used to sport years ago when banana seats were popular. Reaching inside the basket, I moved aside the handkerchief to reveal a cell phone.

"That looks shiny and fun," Olly said.

"Ding, ding. We found the missing cell phone." I conjured up a pair of gloves and pulled out the phone from the basket. "Here's hoping it's not password protected."

It wasn't.

"Lots of texts that night," I said. "Looks like at least two different numbers were trying to reach Selma." I showed Alex the screen. "There's over twenty-seven text messages from this number alone. Basically escalates from 'call me,' to 'you better call me or else,' threats."

"The last is an audio text," Alex said. "Let's hear it."

I pushed the triangle and heard Marvina Darkstone's voice come through loud and clear…making physical threats if Selma didn't come through with the Lunar Blossom. "That's Marvina's voice. Timestamp shows the texts started the night of the full moon around 9:27, and the last text was the voice text at 11:48."

"And then nothing. Why? Because she found Selma and killed her?"

I shrugged. "Maybe. Guess we should go ask Marvina ourselves."

"Do you have something shiny I can have?" Olly asked.

Alex reached inside his pocket and pulled out a dime. Tossing it to Olly, the little otter jumped and snatched it out of the air. *"Thanks! I'll put it in my box of treasures."*

🎋 18 🎋

Hazel Birchwood didn't look any more rested than the last time I'd seen her. Her hair was still in a messy updo, but she'd traded her brown pants and brown top for a monochromatic gray ensemble today. The only splash of color came from her apron—it was coated with bold splatters of reds and greens and purples. A row of paintbrushes lined her waist.

"I didn't know you painted as well," I said.

She motioned us inside. "Here and there. I majored in art history, so I enjoy bringing the techniques I studied into my own works of art." She sighed. "I suppose you're here to talk with Marvina again?"

"We are," I agreed. "This is Sheriff Stone."

Hazel nodded to Alex, and then gave a small, tired smile to Needles. "Marvina is in the living room. She was once again up most of the night and into the early morning hours. She just can't seem to get her latest creation perfect."

I was better prepared for the pitch blackness of the living room this time. Marvina was reclining on the chaise in pretty much the same dramatic fashion as yesterday—reclining, and one arm thrown over her eyes. She was dressed in all black again…the only spot of color on her lips.

They were blood red.

"Marvina," Hazel whispered. "Agent Loci-Stone and her husband, Sheriff Stone, are here to see you."

"Oh, so now I'm invisible?" Needles mused, his wings glowing red and black.

"Tell them to go away," Marvina said, her face still hidden. "I absolutely *cannot* see anyone today. I'm just not feeling it."

"I'm afraid I must insist," I said. "We found Selma Greenleaf's cell phone."

Marvina shot up from the chaise, her short hair flying about her face. "Did you find the Lunar Blossom?"

Hazel sighed. "I've told you over and over again, Marvina. What that horrible woman gave you *wasn't* Lunar Blossom. For all we know, she gave you some kind of poison."

She wasn't far from the truth.

"It allowed me to open my mind and have the creative energy flow from my body," Marvina snapped. "How can that be poison?"

I withdrew Selma's cell phone from the bag I was holding and played the voice text. Marvina's angry voice echoed loudly in the room for everyone to hear. When it was over, I slid the phone back inside the bag. "Do you remember making that call to Selma on the night she was murdered?"

"No."

"Is that your voice, Marvina?" I asked.

Sighing, Marvina reclined back onto the chaise, once again hiding her face. "I suppose it is."

"Were you with her when she made the call?" I asked Hazel. "It was right at midnight."

Hazel shook her head. "I don't remember Marvina making the call, but I could have been in the kitchen brewing some tea. She worked that night until about two."

"Brewing tea or mixing up her next fix?" Needles mused.

"Where is your cell phone now, Marvina?" I asked.

"How am I to know?" Marvina mumbled. "I'm too despondent to remember such trivial things."

"Drama much?" Needles muttered.

"I can call it." Hazel withdrew her own cell phone, slid her finger over the screen, and a few seconds later, the ringing of bells came from a black sweater hanging over the back of a chair situated in front of a roll-top desk.

"Is that your sweater, Marvina?" I asked as Hazel hurried to shut off the phone.

Marvina lowered her elbow just enough to see Hazel pick up the sweater, reach inside the pocket, and shut off the phone. "Yes. That's mine."

"When's the last time you wore that sweater?" I asked.

"How would I know?" Marvina snapped. "I don't even know what day it is now."

Hazel gave me an apologetic smile. "I don't know. Maybe it's been here a couple days."

"When was the last time Marvina left the house?" Alex asked.

Hazel's eyes went wide. "A couple days, I'm sure of it."

"Are you?" I mused.

Hazel glanced back over at Marvina—still lying on the chaise. "Yes."

But we all heard the uncertainty.

"That's as good as saying Marvina's guilty," Needles said.

"I'll need to take the sweater," I said. "For evidence."

Hazel's already pale face went even whiter if that was possible. Hands shaking, she handed me the black sweater. I conjured up an evidence bag and levitated the sweater inside. Hazel then showed us out.

As I climbed into Alex's Blazer, I looked back at the front door. Hazel still had the door open, but she was looking behind her back inside the house. Almost like she wasn't sure she wanted to go back in.

"Let's drop the sweater and phone off at the station for Finn," Alex said. "Then we can finish out the day on the east side of the island."

"Think Finn will find evidence Marvina was out at Luna Lagoon?" I asked.

"If there's any trace evidence or blood splatter to be found, then Finn will find it."

Once the sweater and Selma's cell phone were dropped off, Alex drove us toward the east side of the island to Howling at the Moon to talk with Donald Frasier. We were in the parking lot when my phone rang.

"It's GiGi," I said, sliding my finger over the screen and putting her on speakerphone.

"You're gonna hate this," GiGi said by way of greeting. "I just spoke with Gertrude Anise. She was on the south side foraging under the full moon the other night, and she said she saw Regina Hawthorn out there. She didn't speak to her because she didn't want anything to do with her, but Gertrude said she was sure it was her."

"Crap! What time?" I asked.

"Right before midnight," GiGi said. "Gertrude was about to start her spell work when she saw her."

I groaned. "So it looks like Regina Hawthorn has someone who can corroborate her alibi after all."

"And we all know Gertrude is salt-of-the-earth," GiGi said. "If she said she saw Regina, then she saw Regina."

"Exactly." I sighed. "Man, I was sure with her erratic behavior last night and this morning, she might be good for the murder."

"Sorry to tell you otherwise," GiGi said. "See ya tonight."

* * *

I t was after three o'clock when Alex parked in front of Howling at the Moon. The neon sign flashed "OPEN" in myriad colors as we strolled to the front door. As Alex held it open for me, he ran his hand over the ornate carvings.

"I like the door," he said.

I laughed. "I said the same thing."

Even though the bar was open, no lights were on inside. Instead, Donald seemed to want the natural lighting from the sun spilling through the tinted windows to hold that honor. I didn't figure it was because he was going for a certain feel or ambiance...but more because he didn't want to pay for electricity.

"Well, well, Game Warden," Donald drawled from behind the bar. "Back again for more?" He shifted his gaze to Alex, taking in his sheriff's uniform. "And you brought bigger back up this time. What's the matter? The little witch not feeling well today?"

Needles gave a low growl in my ear, but I simply smiled. "Serena is doing just fine." I glanced around the empty bar. "Where'd your drunk go? I thought maybe he was a permanent fixture in here. You know, make it look like you have people in the seats."

Donald scowled. "Why're you here? To harass me?"

I shook my head. "Nope. No harassing going on here. We just came to ask you some questions about your past, is all."

"So you *have* come to harass me." He held up his hands and motioned around the bar. "I've done nothing wrong."

"You can't always say that, can you?" I mused.

Needles flew up to the beams overhead, leaving Alex and me to deal with Donald Frasier.

"I did my time," Donald said. "That means I have a clean slate now."

Alex leaned against the counter, taking in the empty bar. "Your financials show you don't have long before you'll need to close the bar permanently."

Donald poured himself a splash of bourbon and tossed it back. "Don't see why you should be messing around in my financials. None of your business."

"This is a murder investigation," I said. "Everything is our business."

"I have an alibi for the night Selma Greenleaf was killed," Donald pointed out.

"An alibi no one can corroborate," I said, taking out my phone. "Is this your cell phone number?" I pulled up the picture I'd snapped of the other number on Selma's phone. "Is this you?"

Donald glanced down at the phone. "That's my number. And, yes, I texted Selma that night. Just a friendly reminder I wanted to bid on the Lunar Blossom. Nothing illegal about that."

"This doesn't sound very nice, Mr. Frasier," I said. "You wrote, 'If you try and screw me on this, I will hunt you down and rip out your throat.'" I glanced up at him. "Does that sound like a friendly reminder to you?" When he said nothing, I looked at Alex. "What do you think, Sheriff?"

Alex crossed his arms over his chest. "I think anyone who'd knowingly sell Lupine Elixir, a drug that is both addictive and deadly to his patrons, might think nothing of making threats to someone."

Donald poured himself another drink. "Are you here to arrest me?" He tossed back the drink. "Because if you aren't, then I'm going to ask you to leave. I'm closing up early tonight. I've got a little errand I need to take care of."

19

"**E**verything looks amazing," I said to Mom as I set the cheese tart on the fold-out table.

"It does," Mom agreed, "and with everyone here, Black Forest feels so alive."

I glanced around and smiled. She was right. Alex, Byron, Walt, and Doc were spreading out the last of the blankets, while Grant, Jordan, and Finn entertained the twins. I was helping Mom and GiGi set out the meal while Aunt Starla and Serena worked on the desserts.

When Finn had arrived, she'd informed us she detected blood splatter on Marvina's sweater. She was still running the results through her computer for a DNA match to the blood. When a match was found, her phone would let her know.

A part of me was worried it might just be Marvina's blood since I knew she'd damaged her hand at some point recently.

Alex's cell phone rang, and a huge grin spread across his face. He lifted the phone in the air. "It's Zoie!"

I jogged over to where he stood and waved into the phone. "Hey, Zoie. How were classes today?"

"Great. Only three more months left."

Zoie and her boyfriend, Brick, were currently going through PADA's detectives' training program. Once they graduated, Zoie, Brick, forensic scientist Harlow Grimmson, and Needles would make up a new division in PADA called the Remote Location Team.

"Wish you were here celebrating with us," I said.

"That makes two of us," she said.

I waved goodbye, giving her time alone with Alex. Since Mom and GiGi had most of the food set out, I decided to go talk with Dad. Levitating myself up, I leaned against his trunk.

"I love seeing everyone here."

"As do I, Daughter of my Heart."

"I don't regret the years I spent away from the island working for PADA," I said, "but now, I can't imagine living anywhere else."

"I am pleased to hear you say that."

"Brooke, no!"

At Grant's startled cry, I whipped my head around to see what was going on. Brooke, obviously bored with levitating her brother, Cayden, and all their toys, somehow shifted into her werewolf form and was now chasing two squirrels and one rabbit.

"Grant!" Serena cried. "Grab her!"

Needles drifted down to land on my shoulder. *I told you, Princess. I said it was only a matter of time before those babies burned down Black Forest."*

Dad and I both laughed.

"Relax. There's no fire," I said. "Brooke is just a baby were-wolf chasing some woodland creatures." I bit my lip. "Yeah, even

I can't make that sound sane and commonplace. Poor Grant and Serena."

Giggling with glee, Cayden seemed to be urging his were-sister on with his squeals of delight and clapping.

"Should I go help?" Needles asked.

Grant managed to catch up to his daughter, and just as he was about to snatch her mid-sprint, Cayden waved his arms and levitated Brooke into the air.

Brooke, looking absolutely adorable in her baby werewolf state, giggled as she flipped somersaults in the air. Grant reached up and snatched Brooke, pulling her back down.

"Oh, my goodness, I'm so sorry!" Serena cried out. "Are the animals okay?"

"Fear not, Serena," Dad said. *"No harm will come to the animals or the twins while in Black Forest."*

A dozen or so fireflies flew over to where I sat.

"The babies make me tired!"

"I think Serena is crying!"

"Are all babies like that, Princess?"

"No one feed them sugar water!"

"Babies are a lot of work," I said.

Dad chuckled. *"They are just being babies, my little friends. They will soon grow up, and we will find ourselves looking back at these times and wishing we could relive them. We need to cherish this time with Brooke and Cayden."*

The fireflies looked at each other uncertainly…but Dad was Black Forest King. He wouldn't steer them wrong, even if they didn't understand.

"Of course, Black Forest King!"

"Let us play some more with the babies!"

"Don't let them get your wings, they like to pull!"

"Let's go help Grant and Serena!"

With that, the fireflies zipped away.

"Time to eat!" GiGi called out.

While Grant and the fireflies tried to coax Brooke to shift back into her human form, the rest of us filled our plates with the goat cheese tart, spinach burgers, and fresh fruit salad.

Settling down on an oversized pillow atop one of the blankets, I waited for Alex to join me. Using her magic, Mom poured wine and sent it over my way. Soon, we were all eating, laughing, and telling stories. At one point, the plates were disposed of, and Serena and Aunt Starla passed out the dessert. I was just contemplating a second glass of wine to go with the last of my cherry scone when my cell phone rang.

"It's Hagatha Broomly," I called out. "She must be calling to tell us her exciting news about marrying Dash and Devona." I slid my finger over the icon and put her on speakerphone as everyone quieted around me. "Hey, Hagatha. What's new?"

"Shayla!" Hagatha cried. "You need to come now! I don't know if I can keep Dash alive! And my poor Devona!"

In an instant, Alex, Grant, and I stood as one.

"Where are you?" I demanded.

Hagatha sobbed for a couple of seconds. "Devona's house. Hurry! Dash is badly hurt!"

"We're on our way!" I promised before disconnecting.

"Shayla," Dad said. *"I will call Randor to assist you. Doc and Alex can fly you and Grant to Devona's house. You and Needles can use your magic to keep them alive. Bring them here. We will heal them in Black Forest. Go! We will await your return."*

✿ 20 ✿

I smelled the blood before I saw it…and I heard Hagatha's weeping before I saw her. Doc, Alex, Grant, Needles, and I went into action the minute we viewed the carnage.

"I'll take Dash," Doc muttered. "I can see open wounds."

Dash and Devona lay entwined on the floor. The trail of blood left no doubt Dash had been assaulted elsewhere, but had somehow managed to crawl across the floor to lie next to a broken Devona.

Quite some time ago, Finn Faeton had gone through something similar. We'd been chasing a bad guy on magic carpets, and she'd fallen off and landed on a rocky riverbed. She'd had so many broken and shattered bones, I was sure she'd never be the same.

But then Dad had healed her. It was one of the first times I'd witnessed his awesome power. He'd helped me heal from a gunshot wound once…but to heal broken and shattered bones. Well, that was next-level stuff. So, while it looked bad, I knew Dad could fix Devona.

"Who would do this?" Hagatha demanded, brushing aside her tears. "Why? Because she's a normal? Is someone mad about them dating?"

I shook my head. "No." I laid my hand on her shaking shoulder. "I think Devona saw something she wasn't supposed to. Or, at least, our killer *thinks* she did."

"I'm so confused," Hagatha said. "You're saying this has to do with Selma Greenleaf's murder?"

I nodded. "Yes. Listen, I need to see to Devona."

Hagatha nodded. "Of course. I have yarrow on Dash. I did that before I called you. I figured you guys could get here the fastest." She turned and staggered over to the sofa. "I need to sit before my legs give out, and I fall on my face."

I knew I should tell her to go to another room so she didn't contaminate the crime scene, but I just couldn't force the older witch to walk to a different room.

"From my initial examination," Doc said, "I believe it's Dash who is most critical. Devona looks like she's been dropped from a ten-story window, but there's no outward signs of internal injuries. No swelling in her stomach. Dash, on the other hand, is suffering from internal and external injuries. I need to get him to Black Forest immediately."

"Black Forest King is waiting," Needles said calmly in my ear. *"We just have to get them there. He will make it right, Princess."*

The floor under us vibrated and moved, and I glanced out Devona's window into her backyard in time to see Randor tuck his wings inside his massive dragon body. Unlike Doc, who could shift to a dragon, Randor *was* a dragon. An honest-to-goodness dragon over thousands of years old.

And never had I been so glad to see him.

Wiping away my own tears, I turned to Alex and Grant.

"Alex, you shift and carry Devona. Grant, I want you and Needles to ride Randor back and carry Dash with you. Doc, can Hagatha and I catch a ride back with you?"

"Of course," Doc said.

Using my magic, I carefully levitated Devona in the air and followed Alex outside. Once he was in his gargoyle form, I moved Devona's broken body next to him and lowered her in his arms, careful of his sharp talons. With a nod, he flapped his wings and shot up into the night sky.

"Randor, I need you to carry Dash and Grant back to Black Forest."

Randor pawed at the ground and nodded his massive head. *"Of course, Princess. Whatever you need."*

Ignoring the cries of panic and sorrow coming from the myriad flowers in Devona's backyard—they could sense something was wrong with their beloved mistress—I hurried back inside. By now, Hagatha had regained control over her emotions, and she stood ready to help me with Dash.

"Hagatha," I said gently, "I can get Dash outside. Can you ward the house so no one comes back or can get in?"

"Of course," the older witch replied.

I motioned for Grant to go outside and carefully levitated Dash using my magic. The blood dripping from his body back down to the floor was almost my undoing. Steeling my nerves, I moved him out the door.

I was shocked to see Grant already on Randor's back. I was sure I'd have to levitate him up there as well since the dragon was so big. Like with Devona, I carefully placed Dash in Grant's arms as he sat astride Randor. Needles waggled his wings at me before flying up to sit astride one of Randor's massive wings.

"We will see you back at Black Forest, Princess," Needles said.

When they were up in the air and Hagatha had finished warding the house, I turned to Doc. "I think we're ready."

Shifting into his dragon form, Hagatha and I levitated ourselves onto Doc's back.

"Will she be okay, Shayla?" Hagatha whispered as she wrapped her frail arms around my waist. "Please say she will. Devona is like the granddaughter I never had."

I patted her wrinkled hand. "I promise, Hagatha. Dad and the others will do everything they can for both of them."

True to his word, Dad *did* work his magic. And so did GiGi, Mom, Aunt Starla, and Hagatha. Together, the four powerful witches helped with the aftercare once Dad healed Dash and Devona.

It had taken Hagatha a few minutes to get over the shock of seeing Black Forest King—and hearing him speak in her head— but then she got down to the business of saving Dash and Devona.

Now the two young lovers were resting, thanks to whatever it was GiGi had forced down their unconscious throats. Keeping them knocked out to heal had been Dad's idea. At one point, Dash had stirred, cried out for Devona, and unconsciously started to fight Dad's healing—Dash was so focused on seeing Devona and making sure she was okay. So the decision had been made to keep them asleep and rested.

Like with Finn, Dad had magically healed all of Devona's snapped bones. I'd held Finn as she watched Dad heal Devona and she cried—for both the pain she'd suffered a while back *and* for Devona's pain. She knew what that experience was like.

Now Alex, Grant, Finn, Walt, Needles, and I were sitting around the base of Dad's tree, planning our next move. GiGi, Hagatha, and Mom were watching over Dash and Devona, while Serena, Aunt Starla, and the twins were at Serena's cottage, settled in for the night. Byron, Doc, and Jordan had offered to stay, but we'd thanked them and sent them on their way. Only Walt—the former sheriff—had insisted on staying.

Alex sipped the last of his coffee. "I guess it's safe to say whoever killed Selma Greenleaf also saw Dash and Devona out at Luna Lagoon that night."

"Which was always our fear," I said. "I think we can eliminate Hannah Trueheart and Regina Hawthorn. Their alibis checked out. Plus, I've noticed Regina is left-handed. Seeing as how Selma was hit on the left side of her head, I believe we're looking for a right-handed killer. So I'm good eliminating both women. So now we bring in our remaining four suspects—Ella Greenleaf, Donald Frasier, Marvina Darkstone, and Hazel Birchwood."

"What are you thinking?" Alex asked. "Lay it out for us."

I stood and paced in front of the group, Needles resting on my shoulder. "We know Donald Frasier has a temper and a criminal past. I like him for this because if he could get his hands on what he *thought* was the Lunar Blossom, then his bar wouldn't be in jeopardy of shutting down. I think the alibi he gave us for the time of Selma's murder was a lie. He also told us tonight he was closing down early because he had an errand to run. If he *was* the guy out at the lagoon the other night, then he might have recognized Dash. They're both werewolves. And while I know not all werewolves know each other on Enchanted Island, it wouldn't be hard for him to figure out who Dash was if he just asked around his mostly werewolf bar. Also, as a werewolf, it wouldn't be hard for him to jump an unsuspecting couple and overpower them—especially when one is a normal."

"He just had to take down Dash first," Grant murmured.

I nodded. "Yes. And he has motive and opportunity for both Selma's murder and to attack Dash and Devona."

"And Ella Greenleaf?" Alex asked.

I grimaced. "Ella seems more temper-tantrum thrower than killer, to me. We've seen her throwing things in anger, but the truth is, her magic isn't all that great. She couldn't even hex someone correctly." I held up my hand. "I know she has the most to gain both financially and possession-wise, and because she *is* full of rage and vengeance, she definitely needs to come in to be questioned. I wouldn't put it past her to lash out and do what she did to Dash and Devona in anger. Use her magic to restrain Dash, and then attack them both."

Alex cocked his head and studied me. "But you don't believe she could have gotten the jump on Dash, do you?"

I shook my head. "I don't think so. Even using magic. But she still comes in to be questioned because I've been wrong before."

"And the other two?" Walt asked.

"Marvina Darkstone and Hazel Birchwood," I murmured. "I'll start with Marvina. She's a junkie. Pure and simple. I know the 'enhancements' she uses are considered natural, but she's still an addict. Every time I've spoken to her, she's either been erratic or despondent. I saw the look in her eyes when I mentioned Selma and the Lunar Blossom. She'd do anything to get it, and she left messages on Selma's phone up until the time of Selma's murder demanding the flower. We also found a sweater that belonged to Marvina at her house with possible blood, and Finn is running the DNA found on the sweater now in hopes of finding a match."

"I should be getting that match soon," Finn said. "The program has been running for a couple hours now. I usually get a hit by this time."

I nodded. "Good. On the night of Selma's murder, Hazel gave the same alibi for both her and Marvina—they were at Marvina's house and Marvina painted until two in the morning. But when I questioned Hazel about Marvina's texts and one voice text, she couldn't recall those happening? Why? If they were both home, shouldn't Hazel recall that? I don't think much gets by the stalwart PA."

"Is that why Hazel is a suspect?" Finn asked.

"She knows her employer," I said. "I find it hard to believe Marvina could sneak out of the house without Hazel knowing."

"So maybe they committed the crime together?" Finn asked.

"That's what we need to figure out," I said. "That's why they both come in."

"Can I go?" Finn asked. "I'd like to see this through."

I smiled. "Of course."

"Me too," Walt said. "If that's okay."

"You bet," I said. "Now, here's what I'm thinking…"

Five minutes later, after I broke down the teams, we all headed our separate ways.

❧ 22 ❧

"I'll follow your lead," Finn said as we stepped out of the Bronco and Needles settled on my shoulder.

From the outside, Marvina Darkstone's two-story house looked dark and foreboding. If there was a light on inside, I couldn't see it.

I'd just crossed in front of the vehicle when Finn's phone beeped. "That's the lab." She pulled out her phone, scanned the screen, then shoved her phone back inside her pocket. "It's a match. Blood came back on Marvina's sweater as belonging to Selma Greenleaf *and* Marvina Darkstone."

"Now what?" Needles asked. *"Do you want me to get inside via a chimney?"*

"Give me a minute to think," I said. "By now, Walt and Grant should have Donald Frasier picked up, and Alex should have Ella in custody. Alex could, technically, fly here in less than five minutes."

"Or you, me, and Finn can do this ourselves, Princess."

I nodded. "Yes, but I'd like to have backup, just in case."

Needles huffed, but he didn't argue with me.

I reached for my cell phone, just as GiGi's face filled the screen. "It's GiGi. She's video calling me." I slid my finger over the screen. "I'm about to go get Marvina and Hazel, GiGi. Is it Dash or Devona? Are they okay?"

"They're fine," GiGi said. "It's about something else. I just got off the phone with Beulah Sparkman."

"Okay," I said, trying not to sound impatient. "Who's she?"

GiGi huffed. "She works at Teas, Tinctures & Tonics."

"Oh, right. The elderly witch who does the tonics. I remember her name was Beulah. What about her?" I glanced up at the front door, eager to apprehend Marvina and Hazel, only half listening.

"Beulah said Ella closed down the shop at five tonight and then took her to Enchanted Island Café for a celebratory dinner. Selma's attorney told Ella she gets to keep the house, and there's a little money to inherit as well."

"Okay. We figured Selma would have something in place. That's not really news."

"Just give me a minute," GiGi snapped. "Don't rush me. Anyway, after they finished supper, Ella wanted to go to Boos & Brews for a drink, but Beulah declined."

"I'm going to take a look inside, Princess. I'll be right back."

Before I could call him back…Needles was gone. Leaving just Finn and me by the Bronco.

"Did Ella still go to Boos & Brews?" I asked, somewhat distracted. "I wonder if Alex is having a hard time locating her since she's not at her house?"

"Beulah said the last time she saw Ella, it was after six and Ella was heading to the bar."

I frowned. "You're thinking about the timeline?"

GiGi nodded. "Yep. There's no way Ella had time to walk to the bar, have a drink, and then get over to Devona's house, subdue Dash, and hurt them."

I again glanced up at the darkened house. "We're one step ahead of you, GiGi."

"Beulah did say something else that I thought odd," GiGi continued, as though I hadn't spoken. "She said all throughout dinner Ella bragged about how she lied to you. She actually *did* know who the others were that were bidding on the supposed Lunar Blossom. She'd snooped and found her grandmother's list and memorized the other bidders' names."

"GiGi, I really don't—"

"Throughout dinner," GiGi interrupted, "Ella kept talking about how she was going to go out to Marvina's house and tell her she could supply Marvina with whatever it was her grandmother promised her. She kept encouraging Beulah to put in a good word for her with her granddaughter."

I frowned and motioned for Finn to follow me up to the front door. I'd somehow gotten lost in the conversation with GiGi. "Whose granddaughter? Selma's? Are you talking about Ella?"

GiGi shook her head. "No. *Beulah's* granddaughter. Ella Greenleaf wanted Beulah to put in a good word with her granddaughter so Ella could sell natural enhancements to Marvina."

I frowned over at Finn, then glanced back down at my phone. "Who's Beulah's granddaughter?"

Hazel Birchwood opened the door...still dressed in her gray monochrome outfit, paint-splattered apron, and massively wild hair. "I'm afraid Marvina isn't up for company."

"That's okay," I said, disconnecting the phone and shoving it in my pocket before GiGi could answer. "We're actually here to speak with both of you."

"Is it an emergency?" Hazel asked. "Because if it's not, then

I'll ask you come back later. Marvina has taken a turn for the worse, and she's not really feeling like herself right now. I need to be with her."

I gave her a tight smile and stepped into her personal space, making her back up. "I'm afraid I really must insist, Hazel."

✿ 23 ✿

A loud clatter, followed by a frustrated scream, and then a cry of pain from Needles came from down the hallway.

Hazel sighed. "Marvina is coming down off the Museleaf. I left your porcupine in the living room to watch over her. I guess that didn't work out very well."

Pushing her aside, I jogged down the hallway, half afraid of what I'd find. Either Needles was trying to run the vampire through with his quills and she was putting up one heck of a fight, or Marvina was giving Needles chase around the room.

Neither scenario sat well with me.

I came to an abrupt halt in the darkened living room. It was worse than I thought. Needles was pinned against the wall, unable to move...Marvina's sharp vampire nails impaling his body. The pain etched on his tiny face was nearly my undoing.

"I'm okay...Princess. Any minute now...I'm gonna...run her through...with my quill." His wings looked like a kaleidoscope stuck on high. *"Any minute now."*

Marvina whipped her head around to look at me—at least, I

132

thought it was Marvina—hissing and flashing her fangs. Her chin-length dark hair was gone, and in its place was white-spun strands of stringy hair. Her pupils were red, and her face pale.

She was hardly recognizable.

"I tried to tell you she wasn't feeling like herself," Hazel said.

I whirled around and looked at her. "What have you done?"

"What have *I* done?" Hazel demanded. "I've done my job! I've kept Marvina focused on her painting—no matter the cost!"

I turned back to look at Needles, struggling to reach for a quill while still impaled to the wall, and nearly lost my dinner. "How could I have not seen this?"

"I made sure it was always dark in here," Hazel said calmly. "A little glamour, a little darkness…you never saw it coming. Much like this."

The pain that ripped through my body was five times worse than when I'd been shot with a gun in the shoulder. I screamed… or at least, in my head, I screamed. I wasn't sure anything came out of my mouth.

"Princess!" Needles screamed in my head.

That I heard.

Staggering to my feet, I looked down at the blood oozing from my side and stomach. I couldn't seem to focus. How had I gotten the wound? Why was there so much blood?

"Finn?"

Why I said Finn's name, I don't know. So many thoughts were flooding my brain—Alex, Needles, Dad, pain, Finn.

Hazel laughed. "I already bashed in the fairy's head. As you can tell from Selma's dead body, I'm good at cracking skulls."

"What did you do?" I gasped.

I wasn't sure if I was talking about myself, or Finn.

"Hey, you're the one who went and left your two partners

alone. As far as Finn goes…one good blow upside the head and no more fairy."

I raised my hands, calling up my magic through the pain. If I was going down, by goddess, I'd go down fighting! I sent a wave of magic at Hazel…who laughed and batted it away like an annoying bug.

"Why?" I gasped.

"Why kill Selma Greenleaf? Because she was trying to edge me out. If she became Marvina's supplier, then I wouldn't be needed anymore. My job would be obsolete."

"You're the one who saw Devona and Dash in the lagoon the other night, aren't you?" I pressed my hand against my stomach, trying to stop the bleeding. "You told your Grandma Beulah about the marriage proposal."

"Yes. I'd been following Selma for a week by then. Ever since she came out to the house. I would lace Marvina's drink at night with the drink Selma left, leaving Marvina incoherent. I'd then perform a cloaking spell and track down Selma in the lagoon and watch her. I knew where she kept her secret stashes. I was also pinching a flower here and there to put in Marvina's drinks."

"And Marvina's sweater?" I gasped.

"On the night of the full moon, I drugged Marvina, cut her hand, put the blood on the sweater, and was ready to set her up if need be. I also saw the messages she sent while I was gone and figured that would just be icing on the cake. So I slipped her cell phone inside the sweater pocket too."

She blasted me with a wave of magic…sending me backward and smashing into the fireplace. I'd have cried out in pain…but I didn't have it in me.

"Princess!" Needles cried. *"Fight! I will…fight…as well."*

I shook my head, trying to clear my brain. But it only made

me fall to my knees and throw up. Which immediately made me feel a little better.

"I knew worst-case scenario," Hazel continued, as though my throwing up on the living room floor was commonplace, "Marvina would be arrested for the murder...and I could step in and take her place. It's why I've been mimicking her paintings the last few weeks. I step in, take over Marvina's buyers, and make the money I deserve to be making. I'm the one who went to school and studied! Not her! I've worked for it! I'd appreciate it more! I'm not weak. I won't look under every rock for my next fix to get the job done." She scowled over at Marvina, who was still holding Needles captive against the wall. "Look at her! She's been taking the stuff Selma left. Not the Museleaf, like I told you. Now look at her...totally out of control."

I glanced up at Needles...and rage shot through me! How *dare* Hazel use Marvina to hurt Needles—the protector my dad sent to watch over me in the crib.

For that...Hazel would pay.

Knowing my magic was weak, I drew on my creative side as well. Hazel wasn't the only imaginative person in the room.

"Needles," I panted, *"can you hold on for a few more seconds?"*

"Always, Princess. For you...I would give...my life."

And that was my undoing.

Because I knew Needles was telling the truth. He would give his life for me.

Tears streaming down my face, I focused my eyes on him. *"Do you remember when I was a little girl the game we would play? How you would let me best you?"* I lifted my hand from my stomach and looked at the blood on my hand. *"The silliness?"*

"I do, Princess." Needles gasped. *"I'm sorry, Princess. I don't know...how she got...the jump on...me."*

"I will end this witch, and then Dad will heal us," I promised.

"Of course, Princess." Needles closed his eyes and winced. *"I believe...in you."*

Swiping at my tears, I lifted my hands and send a weak steam of magic to Hazel—who laughed and easily batted it aside again. What she hadn't expected was the rug under her feet to be pulled out from under her...making her fall on her butt.

She jumped up and send a bolt of magic my way.

Which I had expected.

I countered it by sending a wave of magic to the sofa. The couch cushions plumped up to five times their normal size and turned into cartoon-like rubber, sending Hazel's stream of magic right back at her! She staggered and fell to her knees, crying out in pain.

Whispering under my breath, I brought the heavy curtains down and sent them to Hazel—wrapping her body tightly in a cocoon. The fabric bound her movements, rendering her momentarily helpless as she struggled against the plush prison I'd conjured. With Hazel momentarily immobilized, I seized the opportunity to gather my strength to fight the drug-induced vampire.

Staggering to my feet, I drew on the magic from Black Forest King and the witch power on my mother's side. This fight would be a battle of honor.

For me...and for Needles.

Steeling myself, I lifted my hands in the air...but before I could strike Marvina, the room lit up with magic so powerful, it blinded me and dropped me to my knees.

I heard Marvina scream in pain…and Needles cry out in both victory and pain as well.

Looking up, I saw Finn in the doorway.

"Something I never told you," she said, magic pouring out from her body in all directions. "After your dad healed me, I gained these superpowers." She grinned. "I heal quicker now. And my magic is even more powerful."

"Let's bring them down, Princess!" Needles cried, his wings glowing red and purple.

"Let's bring them down," I whispered.

🦁 24 🦁

"I don't know what to say." Devona wiped away a tear and hugged me. "I can't believe everything that's happened in the last seventy-two hours. I got engaged to the man I love, attacked and left for dead for a second time in my life, and now I have magic. Uninhibited, soul-happy magic!" Bursting into tears, she threw her arms around me and squeezed...and I tried not to wince. I was still a little tender. "I can't believe it! I feel so alive! Like all those parts inside me that were dead...are now *alive!*" She stepped back, threw her arms in the air, and twirled. "It's *amazing,* Shayla. This feeling inside me is just...*amazing!*"

Dad's chuckle sounded in my head. *"I am glad you are okay with the extra boost, Devona Flame. I do not understand why, but when I heal other supernaturals, their magic is enhanced. In your case, you have gained the magic that was dormant within you. I hope you are okay with that? Shayla has always spoken highly of you and your training. It shows your true heart, Devona Flame. To give selflessly of your time and energy for something that does not gain you anything. It shows your true character."*

Dad paused. *"But if it is not something you want, I can try to take it back."*

"No way!" Devona laughed and shook her head, clutching my arm. "I wouldn't take back this feeling for anything!"

"Good," Dad said. *"I am sure there will be much speculation from other supernaturals as to why and how you have acquired magic, so I will leave it to you how you explain."*

"Or not explain," I said. "Finn never told me of her added magic."

Devona laughed. "Mine might be a little harder to hide, Shayla."

"True," I said.

"Thank you, Black Forest King," Dash said. "For everything. For healing me, for giving Devona—" He broke off, wrapped his arms around Devona, and cleared his throat. "Thank you sounds so trite. You saved both our lives and gave Devona something she has desired her entire life." He rested his head against Devona's. "Yes. Thank you doesn't seem enough."

"It is more than enough, Dash Stryker. I am pleased you both have healed so quickly."

With one last hug from both of them, the two young lovers waved goodbye to Dad and followed the fireflies out of the clearing. They were escorting Dash and Devona back to the castle where Dash's car was now parked, thanks to Grant.

"That was a wonderful thing you did," I said to Dad as I sat down at the base of his trunk. "Devona is over the moon."

"Like with Grant Wolfe, the magic was there...just dormant. I do not know how to explain it, I only know I can help bring it out. Or in the case of Finn Faeton, I guess I can enhance what she already has."

I laughed and wiped away a tear. "I'll say. It was like Finn was lit up from the inside out. I'd never seen anything like it.

And I'm glad this happened with Devona. It has always been Devona's greatest wish to experience magic." I turned and wrapped my arms around his trunk. "And that's for healing me and Needles. You must be exhausted. I know you try to pretend it doesn't take anything from you…but I know better."

Once Finn had subdued Marvina and called Alex, he'd flown to Marvina's house, ensnared them both in a Binder to take away their magic, called PADA, had Finn stay there, and then flown Needles and me straight to Black Forest. Once again, Dad worked his magic on us and healed us completely.

"You are welcome, Daughter of my Heart."

I ran my hand over his trunk before sitting on the ground. "And Finn! What the heck?" I laughed. "You should have seen her, Dad! She was like this magical fighting warrior! It was awesome!"

"Because you never said anything, I said nothing. I did not realize you were unaware of her added strength."

"Totally unaware." I grinned and leaned back against him. "But totally awesome."

Dad chuckled. *"Agreed."*

We sat in silence for a moment…both of us watching Needles fly through Dad's branches, whooping with glee. Less than eight hours ago, we'd both been seriously hurt, but you wouldn't know it now.

I grinned as Olly and a couple other woodland animals came sprinting into the clearing of Black Forest. "Well, well. If it isn't our local heroes!"

Olly stood on his hind legs and waved his front paws over his head. *"Hello, Princess! Did you hear what we did?"*

I waited until Olly scampered over to Dad's tree before answering. "I sure did, Olly. You guys gave that shifty little werewolf a beatdown."

The errand Donald Frasier had closed down his bar early to run…had been to trek out to Luna Lagoon to look for Selma's supposed stash of Lunar Blossom. When Olly and a couple other woodland animals confronted him, Donald had shifted into his werewolf form and gone after the animals. But they were having none of the bullying, and did something that shocked Donald… they joined forces and retaliated. Donald Frasier was left with a chunk of his ear missing, a broken toe, and a permanent hoof-print on his back.

And no hybrid plant to show for his actions.

"I bet they'll sing songs about our bravery, Princess!" Olly said, his little otter face beaming with pride.

"I suppose they will, Olly." Overhead, thunder sounded. "It's a little early in the season for rain. Usually we don't get storms until April."

"Maybe the rainy season will come early this year," Dad said.

"Let's hope not," I said. "It's always the worst three weeks on the island. All that mud, landslides, and washed away roads."

As if on cue, the sky opened and heavy raindrops beat down from overhead. But Dad was ready. He lowered one of his branches and fanned his leaves over my head, making me laugh.

"I think I'll just stay right here for a while, if that's okay with you, Dad?"

"I am always happiest when you are here in Black Forest, Daughter of my Heart. Never forget that. You are always welcomed, and you are always loved."

* * *

Are you ready for the next book in the series? Then click here and get Deadly Rains. Find out what happens when hurricane season comes early to Enchanted Island, and Tommy Trollman finds a family friend dead.

* * *

Love the idea of a Valkyrie witch teaming up with a Fallen Angel to solve crimes? Then the paranormal cozy series, A Kara Hilder Mystery, should be right up your alley! A spinoff from the A Witch in the Woods, this crime-solving duo not only works for their supernatural town of Mystic Cove, but they also work for the Paranormal Apprehension and Detention Agency—which means they travel undercover to take down bad guys. Click here to read Book 1, *Sounds of Murder*: My Book

What happens when a mermaid-witch detective teams up with a treasure-hunting demigod with a snarky miniature glow-in-the-dark dragon named Glo? Find out in this humorous paranormal cozy series that is yet another spin-off from the A Witch in the Woods. Click here and get book 1, *Tangled Waters,* from the Enchanted Waters Mystery series: My Book

. . .

D o you love the idea of a time-traveling, cold-case solving witch? Then Lexi and her side-kick detective familiar, Rex the Rat, are just what you're looking for! Check out their first stop to 1988 in *Time After Time* My Book

H ave you read the hilarious adventures of Ryli Sinclair and Aunt Shirley? This traditional cozy mystery series is always fast-paced and laugh-out-loud funny. But what else would you expect from Aunt Shirley—a woman who has at least two deadly weapons on her at all times and carries her tequila in a flask shoved down her shirt? Book 1 is *Picture Perfect Murder*! My Book

L ove the idea of a bookstore/bar set in the picturesque wine country of Sonoma County? Then join Jaycee, Jax, Gramps, Tillie, and the whole gang in this traditional cozy series as they solve murders while slinging suds and chasing bad guys in this family-oriented series. First book is *Murder on the Vine!* My Book

O r maybe you're in the mood for a romantic comedy...heavy on comedy and light on sweet romance? Then the Trinity Falls series is for you! My Book

. . .

L ooking for a paranormal cozy series about a midlife witch looking to make a new start with a new career? Then A Witch in the Woods is the book series for you! A game warden witch, a talking/flying porcupine, and a gargoyle sheriff! Check out Book 1, *Deadly Claws,* in this prolific series that has caused myriad spinoffs: My Book

ABOUT THE AUTHOR

Jenna writes paranormal and contemporary cozies. Her humorous characters and stories revolve around over-the-top family members and creative murders. Jenna currently lives in Missouri with her husband, stepdaughter, mother, Nova Scotia duck tolling retriever dog, Brownie, and her tuxedo-cat, Whiskey.

When she's not writing, Jenna likes to attend beer and wine tastings, go antiquing, visit craft festivals, and spend time with her family and friends. Check out her website at http://www. jennastjames.com/. When you sign up for her newsletter, you'll not only receive a free box set, but you'll also be able to keep up with the latest releases! BE SURE TO CHECK YOUR SPAM FOLDER! Other important links:

Author Page: facebook.com/jennastjamesauthor

Jenna's Reading Crew Facebook Page: https://www.face book.com/groups/2787636591248452 Bookbub: https://www. bookbub.com/profile/jenna-st-james

Made in the USA
Monee, IL
15 February 2025

12321171R00085